The Flame

Gayle Trent

ISBN-13: 978-0-9967647-1-1

Grace Abraham Publishing
13335 Holbrook St., Suite 110
Bristol, Virginia 24202

For Tim, Lianna, and Nicholas

1

Beryl raced down the road in her shiny, red Camaro heedless of the stares she was getting. She figured it would've been worse had she been in the minivan she taxied the children around in. It had been part of the bargain-- inheritance, actually--two kids and a minivan. Beryl had always thought she'd have children and possibly...unavoidably...a minivan someday, just not all on the same day...certainly not under the circumstances. But then, she never dreamed she'd be driving at break-neck speed trying to get to a meeting with her nephew's teacher while wearing a yellow catsuit with orange flames, red, thigh-high stiletto boots and an orange and red mardi gras-type mask. She could take the mask off, she guessed, but her hands were gripping the steering wheel so tightly that she couldn't quite pry them loose. Besides, "wherever there is a wrong to be righted, an injustice to be overcome, an oppression to be liberated, The Flame will be there. She alone can scorch evil, char cruelty, sear tyranny and ignite fear in the hearts of even the coldest of criminals."

She screeched to a halt in front of Harper Elementary School, got out of the car and ran inside. She was getting used to running in five-inch heels, though it wasn't something she particularly enjoyed. Not to mention, it was a health hazard. All heels with a height above two and three-fourth inches should come with a warning from the Surgeon General...or at least the Podiatrist General. As if it would make a difference.

1

She neglected to sign in at the office and instead found the room indicated in the note Duncan had brought home from school Friday. The door to the room was open, and Beryl breathlessly bounded in.

"Sorry I'm late," she said to the back of the man putting a model of the solar system onto a bulletin board. She assumed he could be no other than Mr. Terrence E. Goodson, sender of the note that had made her simmer all weekend.

"No problem," the man said, rudely proceeding with the placement of his solar system. "I'll be finished with this in a few minutes."

"I have a life, too, Mr. Goodson. Could we talk while you continue your little...project?"

His broad shoulders stiffened, threatening to rip his blue oxford cloth shirt. Still, he did not turn to look at Beryl. "Had you not been tardy for this meeting, we would have had plenty of time. As it is, I have to finish getting ready for class."

"I'm sorry," she said. "We had some problems on the set this morning, and I was on my way to the dressing room when I realized I had only fifteen minutes to get here."

He shrugged, still placing little planets on the bulletin board. "I had sat aside time for you this morning, and I merely needed to know whether you were coming or not."

"Well, I'm here now. What's this about?"

"I think Duncan is having some sort of whimsical ideation."

"Really." She said it flatly so that it was a statement rather than a question.

"Yes. I heard him telling a classmate that his aunt--you, I presume--is some sort of... superhero." He placed a tiny Jupiter on the board and stood back to survey his masterpiece. "It's not unusual for a child who has endured a tragedy such as Duncan has, but--" He turned at last, and Beryl had the satisfaction of watching his jaw drop. "I...you--" He placed his hands on his trim hips. "Holy Frederick's of Hollywood, Batman, is this some kind of joke?"

"Not at all, Mr. Goodson." Beryl slowly advanced toward him. "You see, I just got off work. As I had fifteen minutes to get here in rush hour traffic, I didn't take time to change out of my costume and into my clothes."

"I see."

"Do you?" Beryl stopped just in front of Mr. Goodson and his bulletin board. "I play 'The Flame' on the local television station's morning show for children. It's not something I'm particularly proud of, but if Duncan is, I'm glad of it. Did you question Duncan yourself before you began psychoanalyzing him?"

"No." His lips twitched as if he were trying to hide a smile. "Please, let's sit down."

Beryl eyed the small desks dubiously.

"You take my chair," Mr. Goodson said with a smile.

If he hadn't made her so angry, Beryl would have found him terribly handsome. She was sure every little girl in his class got up and rushed to school every morning in order to look doe-eyed at "Mithter Goodthon" all day. Wonder if they were learning anything? Yeah, probably so...trying to outdo each other and look smart to Prince Charming here. We all start so early, and it takes us so long to learn better. A handsome face was certainly not going to charm Beryl Madison, though...not unless it was attached to the head of one of her darling nephews. She moved around the desk and took Mr. Goodson's chair.

She removed her mask and laid it on the corner of his desk. "Where do you keep your paddle?"

"We don't paddle anymore, Ms.--"

"Madison." She sat back in the chair. "Darn."

His eyebrows shot up as he sat on the opposite corner of the desk. "About Duncan. I didn't question him. I, of course, knew about his parents' death, and I merely wanted to meet with you to see if you'd noticed any odd behavior."

"Odd? No. He still grieves for his parents. I certainly don't consider that odd. I doubt that's something he'll ever get over entirely. But he's adjusting. He, his brother, and I are making a life together."

"And how has this affected you, Ms. Madison?"

"How would it affect you, Mr. Goodson, to wake up one morning to the news that your sister and brother-in-law had died in a car accident and that you were now responsible for their two children?"

"Please call me Terry." His voice had softened with sympathy. "To be completely honest, I don't know how it would affect me."

"I can assure you that it would--" She gestured toward the newly completed bulletin board with her thumb. "Turn your little solar system upside down. But the most important thing to remember is how this tragedy has uprooted the lives of two precious little boys for whom I'm now responsible." She linked her hands behind her head and plopped her feet up on the desk. Beryl Madison could never have gotten away with a flippant gesture like that...but The Flame could. The Flame could get away with most anything.

"Would you like to talk about my childhood now, Dr. Freud?" she continued. "To determine how I might weather this storm...whether or not I'll be able to bear the weight of this unexpected responsibility?"

"No. I'm sorry you mistook my intentions." Eyes surprisingly similar to the color of his shirt gazed at her coolly. "I have a responsibility to these children, too, Ms. Madison. When I think one of them might have a problem, I do what I can to help. At times the problem is non-existent, but at times it's very real; and if I don't get involved, I will have let that child down. Sometimes there's no one to care, so I have to do what I can from the sidelines."

Beryl was looking down at the desk. Terry leaned over and lifted her chin with his index finger. The slight touch sent chills through her.

"Have you ever tried to develop a child's self-worth after he or she has been beaten down for six or seven years by neglectful or abusive parents?"

"No." The word emerged from Beryl's lips as a whisper. She swept her feet off the desk.

"Then after a year, you have to let that child go, hoping you gave him or her a little something to build on." He stood abruptly. "I'm sorry I offended you with my concerns, Ms. Madison."

"I'm sorry." She, too, stood. "I just--" To her horror, tears sprang to her eyes. "You'd think after six months, I'd have this Mommy stuff down pat, but I haven't yet." She looked up at the ceiling and blinked the tears away, daring them to fall while she was attempting to appear so tough. "I took your note as an insult to Duncan."

"I probably should've spoken with him before consulting you, but I didn't want to make him feel as if he'd done anything wrong."

"You were right. You've obviously had much more experience with this type of thing than I have."

He smiled, and Beryl knew that if she were a seven-year-old girl in this class, she'd race to school every morning to see "Mithter Goodthon a.k.a. Printh Charming." And she'd sit on the front row with her chin in her hands and gaze at him adoringly. Good thing she wasn't seven.

"For the record, I think you're doing great," he said. He looked her outfit up and down. "So you're 'The Flame', huh?"

"Uh-huh." She nodded. "Yeah…."

He took a step toward her. Beryl nearly took a step back but held her ground. The Flame never backed down from a challenge, no matter how daunting. And there was an unmistakable challenge in Terry Goodson's eyes.

He reached out and took one of her red curls between two of his long fingers and followed its path as it curved to her shoulder. "Suits you."

"Thanks."

Beryl finished binding the coloring book she was working on, gathered up the rest and shoved them under the couch as she heard the school bus coming. She and Raife, her makeup man/hairdresser/jack-of-all-trades, made *The Flame* coloring books and storybooks and sold them at local stores in order to supplement their incomes. The station required only a ten percent fee for using their "action figure" so for every book they sold for a dollar, she and Raife got forty-five cents each, sans overhead. Harcourt Brace by no means, but every little bit helped.

She stood, dusted off her khaki shorts and opened the door just as the bus stopped in front of the house. Duncan descended the bus steps looking terribly small to Beryl as he wrestled his backpack onto one shoulder. She fought the urge to go help him. She'd learned from experience that not even The Flame could get away with that kind of nonsense without making Duncan ashamed and feeling as if he'd lost face somehow. Everybody is afraid to appear weak. Beryl understood that. So she merely stood in the doorway and waited.

"Hi, babe," she said softly as she opened the door for him.

"Hi."

"Did you have a good day at school?"

"Yeah."

"What'd you do?"

"Nothin'." He dropped the heavy bag on the floor, apparently relieved to be rid of it at last.

After the bus rounded the corner and was out of sight, she dropped a quick kiss on his head. "I went by and talked with Mr. Goodson this morning."

Duncan shrugged and walked to the kitchen.

"You haven't done anything wrong or anything," Beryl assured him. "He just didn't know I was The Flame, and when he heard you talking about it--"

"He thought I was nuts."

"Pretty much, yeah. I was running late and had to go to meet with him in my costume, so now he knows."

Duncan laughed, sitting down at the table. "Your cover's blown, Aunt B."

"Ah, well. I guess it's okay as long as he isn't some criminal mastermind." She flicked his nose with her index finger. "We're having lasagna for dinner, so I didn't make you a snack. Let's go on and pick up Dominic at the day care so we can hurry back here and have supper."

Duncan's dark eyes widened. "You're fixing supper?"

"I'm putting it in the oven. Grandma made lasagna a few days ago, and at the same time, she put this one together and put it in the freezer for us. She dropped it by earlier today. All I have to do is heat it up."

"Great! Let's go!"

Beryl swiped the minivan keys off the table, and she and Duncan headed out the backdoor. Cooking was not something she was taking to very well. In fact, it was not something she was taking to at all. Raife had been trying to teach her the basics, but she couldn't even master those. Both she and Raife were beginning to think that she was beyond help. Beryl had given up all hope of ever learning to do more than microwave a frozen dinner, and though he hadn't come right out and admitted it to her yet, she could see that Raife was nearing that conclusion himself.

Beryl had been affectionately known as "The Cereal Queen" before the kids came to live with her because that's mainly what she lived off of. Her pantry was stocked with the breakfast cereals, the cereals that were more of a lunch or dinner entrée, and, of course, the chocolatey or fruity dessert cereals. She was a cold cereal connoisseur. And that was fine for a single woman, but not so good for a working "mom" raising two growing boys.

"I told Grandma to call us in the next day or so if Grandpa is up to it, and we'll go over and visit them," Beryl told Duncan on the drive to the pre-school Dominic attended.

"Grandpa's funny."

"He used to be...in a different way than he is now. He used to make jokes and funny faces to make us laugh all the time...." Beryl's voice trailed off. It was heartbreaking to see her father in the state of dementia he was so often in these days. The doctor suspected Alzheimer's. What a thief. Gone was the man who'd held her as a child...helped her learn to ride a bike...taught her to waltz...made her laugh when she was afraid. In his place was a child who didn't have the capabilities of three-year-old Dominic. Yet, sometimes, she saw a glimmer of mischief or understanding in his eyes that reminded her that he wasn't completely gone.

She glanced over at Duncan. He was so like his father...dark complexion, raven hair, and deep brown eyes. He was a beautiful child...mature and thoughtful...sometimes brooding and remote since his parents died...but Beryl thought he was actually handling everything remarkably well.

"How are you?" she asked him.

"Fine. How are you?"

She smiled. "I just--" She reached over and ran her hand over his hair. "I love you, Duncan."

"Love you, too, Aunt B. Anything wrong?"

"Nah. Just feeling a little weird after talking with Mr. Goodson, I guess. And I want you to know I'm here for you...to help you in whatever way I can...always."

The awkwardness between them lifted as they drove into the parking lot at The Little Rascals Preschool. She and Duncan got out of the car, and Beryl could hardly restrain herself from sprinting inside at the anticipation of Dominic unabashedly running to throw himself into her arms. True to form, he did just that. She laughed as she hugged his warm little body.

Dominic was--to look at--definitely his mother's child. He had the same dark hair and eyes as Duncan, but he was fair and his features were those of August. Though he was sometimes sad and missed his mommy and daddy, and though he couldn't understand why they had to "go away for a while," his happy go-lucky, devil-may-care attitude was unquenched. Dominic plowed through life wide open and wouldn't recognize a consequence if it popped him on the nose. He'd inherited that from his mother, too.

Dominic planted a wet kiss on her cheek, drawing Beryl back to the present. "Hi, Aunt B-B head!"

"Hi, yourself, Boo Diddle Dumplin'!"

Dominic giggled. "You're silly."

Beryl sat him down and he hugged Duncan.

"Let's go," Duncan said. He'd already gathered up his brother's stuffed ape, Harvey, and his blanket. "We're getting lasagna for dinner that Grandma made."

"Yay!"

"If you eat your lasagna well," Beryl told them, "I'll make you some chocolate chip cookies."

Duncan and Dominic rolled their eyes at each other.

"Slice and bake," she said.

They let out a collective sigh of relief.

Tuesday morning, Beryl sat at her desk peering into a small mirror making sure she'd wiped away all traces of The Flame's makeup before becoming her alter ego, Audit Woman. She often wondered what some poor taxpayer would say if she had to run in to perform an audit the way she'd ran into Terry Goodson's office yesterday. The poor thing would probably scream and run.

She heard the telltale click of Nancy's heels coming down the hall, slipped the mirror back into her desk drawer and was studying a balance sheet when Nancy gave a perfunctory knock on her doorframe.

"Yes?" Beryl looked up. You're looking foreboding as always.

"Clark Samuels called in sick today." The tone of the older woman's voice suggested she didn't believe Clark was being truthful about his illness. This was, however, Nancy Carruthers' modus operandi--guilty until proven innocent...and then still guilty. "Here." She thrust two of the files she carried at Beryl. "Can you do these audits today?"

"Sure." Beryl nodded, smiling at her supervisor's gloomy visage.

Nancy allowed her lips to spread in what might have been a smile, but knowing Nancy as she did, Beryl doubted it. She turned and left the office in her usual "If-It's-Tuesday-It's-Navy" suit, taking away the little black storm cloud that followed her. On Wednesday, Nancy wore gray in the same nondescript style, and Thursday, she went all out and wore a beige suit with a floral print shirt. Beryl had no idea what Nancy wore every Monday and Friday of her life, as those two days were Beryl's days off. She was unfortunately only part-time.

She and a woman named Hilary (with whom Beryl communicated via notes but had never actually met) were in a pilot job-sharing program. Beryl worked three days, and Hilary worked two. According to Nancy, Hilary loved the flexibility and time at home the job-sharing program afforded her. Loosely translated, Hilary was loaded and didn't have to work for a living. Inability to get on with the local office of the Internal Revenue Service full-time and the ever-dangling carrot of "a possibility of something opening up soon" is why Beryl had become The Flame and an expert at making coloring books. Part-time didn't pay the bills, and no other job was as accommodating as The Flame--an hour in the morning and she was out of there. Ah, well, some people would give their eyeteeth for experience like this. Sure, they would. Some people were idiots.

Beryl looked at the top file. This time her smile was genuine. The name on the file was Terrence E. Goodson.

GAYLE TRENT

2

Terry raised his eyebrows skeptically at the tiny office building shoved into the corner of an old, now almost empty, strip mall. You'd think the government would do better for one of its own...but then, this was the Internal Revenue Service. Not even politicians care for this poor relation of the family. He took a deep breath and resolutely strode into the building.

"I have an appointment to see Clark Samuels." Terry wondered if the receptionist really looked that dour or if it was only his imagination.

"He's out sick today," she said. "Another auditor will be handling your case. I'll let her know you're here."

Your case. She made it sound like he was already under arrest for tax evasion...like he was the next Al Capone...only worse. *Sing-Sing, here I come.*

"She'll see you now," the receptionist told him. "Turn right and go down the hall. Hers is the last office on the left."

Terry followed the receptionist's terse directions. As he got to the office, his auditor rose from her desk with her hand outstretched for a handshake.

"Good morning, Mr. Goodson," she said.

Terry shook her warm hand briefly and took note of the fact that her nails were long and red. That went against the stereotyped IRS agent he'd envisioned, but then so did everything about this woman. In fact, every cell in his body was registering recognition and attraction to her. Maybe it was some sort of sadomasochistic thing--being drawn to one's auditor. Terry sat in the chair she indicated as she pushed the door closed.

"Have we met?" he asked.

She laughed, a low husky rumble that gave him goose bumps...the good kind. "Normally, I'd put that down to a lead-in for some type of come on, Mr. Goodson, but in your case, yes, we have. We met yesterday morning to talk about my nephew Duncan."

Terry's eyes widened. "You're Beryl Madison? The Flame?"

"The one and only." The smile still lingered in her voice. "Though I'd appreciate your not broadcasting my secret identity here. I have an image to maintain, you know."

Terry returned her smile. "Ah, yes, and you never know where agents of the villainous underworld might lurk, do you?"

"No, you don't. One might be right under our noses even as we speak."

"But the Flame is here. She alone can scorch evil, char cruelty, sear tyranny, and ignite fear in the hearts of even the coldest of criminals."

Beryl sat down at her desk and quirked a brow at him. "You didn't tell me you were a fan of the show."

"I wasn't until yesterday. I have to say, you certainly present a different picture from the one you presented yesterday morning," Terry mused. Beryl's long, red-gold hair was pulled up and away from her face and into some sort of intricate chignon at her nape. Rather than a yellow catsuit, she wore an almost conservative hunter green business suit--almost conservative because it was just a bit short, but Terry didn't mind the generous view of Beryl's legs at all. "So, this is your 'Clark Kent' persona?"

"In a way. This is my part-time job...which I'm hoping to one day make full-time, so 'The Flame' can retire."

"You could never allow the Flame to retire."

"Why not?"

"You'd miss the excitement too badly."

"Thank you for that insight, Dr. Freud."

"Besides, what would the good citizens of Harper do?" Terry gave her a Bruce-Willis-smirk. "We'd fall prey to the denizens of evil, that's what. And after they'd gained control of Harper, they'd take control of the entire United States of America and eventually…" He took a deep, dramatic breath. "The world."

Beryl inclined her head and got to the business at hand. "I hope that briefcase contains the supporting documentation for your return."

"Of course."

"Then let's get busy."

Terry grinned. "Oh, yes…let's."

Beryl let that pass without comment and began pouring over the tax records.

S everal minutes and about two feet of calculator tape later, Beryl looked up at Terry and said, "You're not gonna believe this."

Terry groaned. "Be gentle. This is my first time."

"We owe you."

His eyes sprang open like a set of faulty window shades, and his jaw dropped. "You're kidding. I didn't think that was possible."

"Oh, it's possible…just not very likely." She turned the form on which she'd been recalculating his return toward him. "See? Just thirty dollars…but thirty dollars is thirty dollars."

"It'll make a dent in a dinner tab," Terry said. "What do you say?"

Beryl smiled. "I'm afraid Ms. Carruthers, my superior, would think of that as a bribe."

Terry leaned forward conspiratorially. "What Ms. Carruthers doesn't know won't hurt her."

"Shhh," Beryl warned, raising an index finger to her raisin-tinted lips. "I'm going to get fired. We're having too much fun, and the government never allows that. And when they see that the government owes you, they'll think I staged it for sure."

Terry looked hurt. "And you didn't?"

"Of course not. And anybody who recalculates this will see the same thing. The only thing that made the computer kick this return out was the jump in income for two consecutive years followed by the decrease the following year." She flipped her hands palms up. "That was simply because you received the inheritance from your uncle, invested wisely, and then your stock took a dive."

"Can't win 'em all."

"All your forms were filled out properly, except that you didn't carry one of your deductions over to your 1040. No mishandling of funds whatsoever."

Terry scoffed. "If anyone mishandled funds, it was Bob March stealing from my uncle's estate."

"Bob March?"

"Yeah. You know him?"

"I sure do. He's the T. V. station's attorney...and he handled my sister and brother-in-law's estate. Do you really think he's dishonest? Or do you think he simply didn't know what he was doing?"

"He just strikes me as a smarmy character, that's all." He shrugged. "I was suspicious of some of the expenses in the final accounting, but when I asked him about them, he explained them away with the ease of someone who's had a lot of practice."

"I see." Beryl picked up her pencil and began twirling it through her fingers.

"Did you have any trouble with him?"

"No. Come to think of it, I never even looked at Ron and August's final accounting." She gave him a self-depreciating grin. "Pretty bad thing for an accountant to admit, huh? But I trusted Bob, and I...I just didn't check it."

"It's probably nothing. I'm probably blowing things out of proportion."

"Maybe." But Beryl's mind had raced back to the time of August and Ron's deaths and was replaying every conversation and meeting she'd had with Bob March. Come to think of it, he was a smooth operator, but did that make him guilty of anything?

"Hey," Terry said, interrupting her train of thought, "it's more than likely that I did overreact. I'm not familiar with inheritances and final accountings and all that." He looked at his watch. "Want to grab some lunch?"

"Uh...I really can't. I was serious about Ms. Carruthers. If we're seen leaving together after I've just completed your audit--"

"So we won't leave together. Accidentally meet me on the other side of town at Mahoney's. Can you do that?"

"Yeah," Beryl said with a slow smile. "That's doable."

"All right." Terry returned her smile.

Mahoney's was one of Beryl's favorite places to eat. She didn't get a chance to go there often since it strained her lunch hour to get there and back within the required time, but today she couldn't resist the alluring combo of Mahoney's and Terry Goodson.

She walked into the small delicatessen and spotted Terry immediately even though his back was to the door. She went over, pulled out the ladder-back chair opposite him, and sat down.

"Why, aren't you Terry Goodson? My nephew's second-grade teacher?" she asked.

"I sure am! Since we're both here, do you care to join me?"

"I already have." She propped her elbows on the red and white checked tablecloth and smiled. "Have you ordered yet?"

"No, I was waiting for you." He held a menu out toward her.

She shook her head. "No, thanks. Don't need it."

A waitress in a white shirt and pants covered by a poppy colored apron walked over to take their order. Terry perused the menu once more before deciding on the club sub and a soda. Beryl brightly ordered the chicken parmesan sandwich and a raspberry iced tea.

As the waitress took their order back to the kitchen, Terry leaned across the table and eyed Beryl speculatively. "You know, you have the greenest eyes. Is that why your mother named you Beryl?"

"Thanks, and I guess that was part of it. Now, what were you really going to say before you decided to stall a bit?"

He laughed softly. "You read minds, too. Interesting. Has Duncan mentioned the scout troop camping trip to you?"

"Yes."

"Has he mentioned we're short one chaperone?"

"Yes."

"It's next Saturday, you know. If we don't find someone soon, we'll have to cancel." He cocked his head. "How do you like camping, Beryl?"

She emphatically shook her head no.

"We could use a woman on the trip."

She continued shaking her head.

"Someone to give us guys a different take on things...you know, a woman's point of view. Someone to mother the boys if they get scared or hurt...not that anyone will get hurt, of course, but say, scrape a knee. No one has that healing touch quite like a woman."

"No, thank you."

"A softer, prettier voice to lend to campout sing-a-longs…a more adept cook…."

Beryl laughed. "You don't know what you're saying there. I've already said no."

"Why?"

"For one thing, Duncan has a little brother."

"Yes. Dominic. I know."

"I can't leave him with anyone for the weekend, and I--"

"So bring him with you. You'll have your own cabin, and Dominic can either stay with you or he can stay in my cabin with me and be like one of the guys, whichever he prefers. It'll make him feel good to be hanging out with the big boys."

Again, Beryl shook her head. "I'm afraid he wouldn't be able to keep up, that he'd be afraid, that he'd try to do things he's not capable of simply because the others were doing it…. No, Terry, I don't think it's a good idea."

"I do…and I'm the psychologist, remember?"

Beryl arched a brow. "When I called you Dr. Freud I was being completely and vehemently sarcastic. You do realize that, don't you?"

"No! You were? Really?" He winked. "I have had some child psychology, you know, and I believe it would be good for Dominic."

"And what about Duncan? How will he feel that he looks to the other guys with his baby brother tagging along?"

"But how will he look to the other guys with The Flame herself tagging along?"

"Not The Flame--his aunt, the only woman on the trip."

"Afraid you can't be cool enough to appeal to the guys?"

"I can be cool enough to appeal to anyone. That's not the issue here." Beryl leaned back in her chair. "Why do you want me on this trip so badly?"

"Maybe I just want you so badly."

"Well, that pushes it over the top for a definite no."

Terry chuckled. "I wasn't planning on throwing you onto your back and accosting you on the down-river rafting excursion, or anything. I only meant that I wouldn't mind getting to know you better."

Beryl knew she was on dangerous ground. She studied the strong curves of his lips and wondered how it would feel to be locked in a hungry kiss with those lips…held against that muscular body….

"I don't think you'd mind getting to know me better either," he said softly.

She started guiltily. "I--" As she faltered for something to contradict his statement, the waitress arrived with their food.

Beryl immediately sank her teeth into the succulent chicken sandwich and glanced at her watch. She really needed to get back to work soon…and away from this man.

Terry chose to stare at her rather than to eat which made Beryl even more uncomfortable. Making women flustered was probably something he did as a hobby--he certainly had an aptitude for it. Beryl dabbed at the corners of her mouth with a napkin as she swallowed.

"Aren't you going to eat?"

"Of course. I do hope you'll reconsider coming on the camping trip. The boys do need another chaperone, and I assure you that I'll be a perfect gentleman."

Choosing not to comment, Beryl continued eating her lunch. Terry followed suit. When Beryl had finished, she glanced at her watch again and hastily stood.

"I'm sorry to be rushing off," she said, "but--"

Terry stood up, and put a hand on her waist. Beryl stiffened. What was he doing? Did he intend to kiss her? Would she try and stop him if he did?

He retrieved his napkin and wiped her chin. "Couldn't let you go back to work with a smudge of sauce on your chin. Ms. Carruthers wouldn't like that at all, would she?"

"No." Beryl smiled. "She certainly wouldn't."

Terry released her, and they said their good-byes.

Beryl was still looking bookish and reserved, in her opinion, when she arrived at school to pick up Duncan. She was, of course, driving the brown minivan, which suited her IRS persona much better than the Camaro. She pulled up behind the parade of other minivans, station wagons, and sedans gathering up children before the buses moved into place.

Duncan spotted her and sprinted to the van.

"Hi, handsome," she said with a wink. "Going my way?"

"Yeah." He slumped into the seat and fastened his seatbelt.

"What's wrong, cutie pie? Have a bad day?"

He shrugged. "Coach Phillips told us during gym today that we might not be able to go on the camping trip next Saturday."

"Oh?" The inevitable settled over Beryl like a thick, scratchy wool blanket. In the middle of July.

"There's not enough chaperones."

Out of the corner of her eye, Beryl saw Duncan's lower lip quiver.

"All right. Mr. Goodson asked me about being a chaperone, but I declined. I was afraid you'd be embarrassed if I went. But--"

"You'll do it! You'll be a chaperone! Wow, thanks!"

It was amazing how the look of sheer dejection had been replaced with sheer joy.

"We'll have to take Dominic," she said.

"That's okay." He didn't look quite so thrilled with this one, but it appeared he'd live with it and make the best of it in order to get to go camping with his scout troop.

"He and I might not be able to keep up with you guys in doing everything, so we might strike out on our own some. Is that okay?"

"Sure!"

"I'll call Mr. Goodson and--"

In one fluid movement, Duncan grabbed up the cell phone and retrieved the phone book from the glove compartment. He looked up Mr. Goodson's home number and dialed it. Beryl knew she should be proud of him for being only seven years old and so skilled, but couldn't he have at least given her time to get used to the idea of being a chaperone? Not to mention giving her time to get used to the idea of phoning Terry Goodson. It was ringing when Duncan handed the phone to her.

"Hello."

"Hel--"

"This is Terry Goodson," the recorded voice continued, "I'm unable to come to the phone right now. Please leave a message at the beep."

"Hello, Mr. Goodson. This is Beryl Madison. I...Duncan..." She knew she was running out of time and didn't want the machine to cut her off while she was stammering like a halfwit. "I'll be a chaperone."

She ended the call and handed the phone back to Duncan.

"Thanks, Aunt B," he said earnestly.

She gave him a wooden smile and wished she could slap August for dying and leaving her with responsibilities she was neither ready for nor equipped to handle.

"I'll be going up in the school bus," Duncan said. "So you can come in the Camaro, right?"

"I guess I can."

"And can you wear really short shorts?"

"Duncan!" She gaped at him then quickly turned her attention back to the road. "Why would you want me to do that?"

"Well, then you'd look like one of Beyonce's dancers, and all the guys would think you're really cool."

She wished she could slap Ron, too.

After she and Duncan picked Dominic up from day care, they went to see Grandma and Grandpa. The boys were thrilled, and Beryl was, too. Although it was depressing to see her dad in his current condition, it was important to be with him; and Beryl always looked forward to seeing her mother. Molly was the most energetic, optimistic "old lady" Beryl had ever run across. Ashamed of her plain name for the majority of her life, Molly Madison had hung Beryl Anastasia and August Penelope on her daughters. *Gee, thanks, Mom.* But then, Beryl had never complained about having a plain name.

When Beryl pulled into the driveway of her childhood home, Molly was on the front porch waiting for them. A petite woman with straight gray hair and hazel eyes, her clothes always seemed to be too big. Today she was dressed in jeans, a blue sweatshirt, and the ever-present running shoes. She never wore makeup--she had no time for such frivolities--and Beryl was probably the only one who would deem her a beauty queen, but she had a radiance that exuded in everything she did. Molly rushed to the van to kiss Duncan and to extricate Dominic who sat with his arms outstretched from his car seat expectantly.

In the midst of the exuberant reception for her grandchildren, Molly called a greeting to Beryl. "Hi, sweetheart. I've got a meatloaf in the oven, and it'll be ready in a few minutes."

"Thanks. Where's Dad?"

"Sitting in front of the T.V." She turned her attention to the boys who were running toward the house. "Be careful that you don't fall on those porch steps, boys. Do you want to visit with Grandpa or help me out in the kitchen?"

"We'll help you, Grandma," Duncan said.

"Yeah!"

The two boys raced into the house with Molly at their heels. Beryl wandered inside, slipped off her shoes, and padded downstairs to the den where her father was watching a Family Feud rerun. She studied his profile for a moment. He was still a handsome man. His dark hair was now starkly white and it seemed he had aged two decades in two years. She remembered how strong he'd been...how hard he'd worked at the furniture factory and at home as well...how he'd seemed unafraid of anything.

"Hi, Daddy," she said softly as she leaned over and kissed his sallow cheek.

He tore his trance-like gaze from the television and studied Beryl. "You sure are a pretty girl, Molly. How'd I get so lucky?" He patted her hand, and she sat down on the chair beside him.

"Thank you. Is this a good show?"

"He keeps kissing all those people. Don't know how he gets by with kissing those women. Their husbands are right there."

"I guess he's just being friendly, Daddy."

"The stock market is up three points. That's a good sign."

"Uh-huh." Beryl didn't keep up with the stock market, so she didn't know what it was doing. She supposed her father was right, although she wouldn't have bet the farm on it. "Daddy, remember when I was little and we had that dog named Cisco?"

He laughed. "Cisco Kid! Sure, I remember. That was the stupidest hound I've ever seen."

"He wasn't very bright, was he?" Beryl joined in his laughter.

"No, he wasn't; but you and August loved him anyway. You two scamps would dress up like cowgirls and tie a red bandana around that old dog's neck and pretend he was the bad guy."

"That's right. We did."

"Where is August?"

Beryl hesitated only for a second. "Home."

"Upstairs getting ready for a date, I reckon. You're gonna have to keep closer tabs on that girl, Molly. You let her get by with too much."

"I know," Beryl whispered, sorry that the moment of recognition had passed.

Molly called that dinner was ready. Beryl asked her father if he was going upstairs, but he was now staring at the television in zombied silence. Beryl sighed and went upstairs.

"How's he doing?" Molly asked.

Beryl shrugged. "Pretty good. Dinner smells great."

"I hope it will be." She nodded toward the table so that Beryl would notice that it had been set.

"Wow! Who set the table? It looks super."

"Me!" yelled Dominic.

"And me," declared Duncan. "I set out the plates and glasses."

"And I did fork and poons," Dominic said proudly.

"You both did a fantastic job," Beryl said.

Suddenly the boys' eyes widened. They were looking at something behind Beryl.

"What?" Beryl asked, turning to see what they were looking at. When she saw, she closed her eyes.

Her father was strolling through the kitchen wearing an old red wig she and August used to wear for Halloween and when they played dress-up. He sat down, picked up his knife and fork and waited expectantly.

"Mom, where'd he find that old thing?" Beryl whispered.

"Who knows?" She grinned and cocked her head. "He looks like Jimmy Stewart playing Howdy Doody."

"Mama!" Despite her best efforts to the contrary, Beryl burst out laughing.

Relieved that the tension was broken and that they, too, could laugh at "funny Grandpa", the boys hooted with laughter.

"Oh, Mama, this is terrible. How could we stand here and make fun?"

Molly shook her head. "We're not making fun, sweetheart. We're making the best of what we have to deal with. If we didn't laugh once in a while, we'd all go insane. Besides, maybe he's trying to make us laugh. He always used to, you know." She went over and kissed her husband's cheek, swiping the wig off his head. "That was a good one, Ralph. You silly thing."

"Yeah. You silly Grandpa," Dominic said.

Beryl watched her father smile brightly, obviously pleased to be the center of attention whatever the reason. With two wild children around, his time in the spotlight was short-lived.

"Hey, Aunt B," Duncan said. "Do you think initials are cool?"

"Sometimes," Beryl answered carefully. "Why?"

"Well, I thought maybe at camp instead of calling you Aunt B, me and all the guys could call you BM. What do you think?"

3

As Raife applied Beryl's makeup the next morning, Beryl confided to him that one of her clients suspected Bob March of mishandling some estate funds.

He turned her chin this way and that, and then picked up a lip brush and applied a coat of clear gloss over her bright red lips. "There. That's better...not so cakey now. Your lips are chapped. Have you been licking them? Or has someone else?"

Beryl scoffed. "What do you think about March?"

He picked up a comb and prepared to pull her hair into what he called the Flame Fount. "Bob March mishandling funds? Girlfriend, that's old news."

Beryl winced as he pulled her hair a bit too tightly. "You think it might be true then?"

"It wouldn't surprise me in the least. What does surprise me is that you've not heard rumors about him before now."

"So you had? And you let my mother hire him for August's and Ron's estate?"

Raife shrugged, shook his shaggy dark ringlets out of his eyes, and wound a yellow cloth-covered elastic band around the hair he'd gathered at the top of Beryl's head. "I figured surely he wouldn't screw you...or your family. He knows you." He arranged the hair spouting from the fount over Beryl's shoulders and then tied her mask in place. "I give you," he said in the exaggerated deep voice he used for the voiceovers at the beginning and end of the show, "*The Flame*."

"Thank you," Beryl said. "Thank you very much. Cue cards ready?"

"Yep."

As if on his own cue, Joe the producer called, "Quiet on the set, people! Beryl, get into position. Raife, get ready to do the lead-in. In five, run the theme. Four...three...two...one." He pointed to a sound man, and the music--which sounded a lot like a cross between the theme from "Phantom of the Opera" and "It's a Small World" began to blare.

Thus began another episode of "The Flame."

The music softened, and Raife said, "When we last saw The Flame, she was facing grave danger at the hands of Wild Man who'd thrown her into a pit with the ferocious...and hungry... white wolf. Is this the end for The Flame? Or can she possibly escape? What will she do?"

The music ended and Camera One zoomed in on Beryl who stood facing the ferocious--and hungry, mind you--white wolf. The white wolf was actually a German Shepherd that was neither ferocious nor hungry and was watching Beryl with his tail wagging merrily as if to say, "Come on, let's play."

Yet, Beryl cringed up against the wall of the pit as if her life was about to come to a horrible end. She scanned the walls of the pit looking for something...anything...to help her escape. Camera Two followed suit. There on the side of the pit a rock jutted out just enough for The Flame to lasso it with her flame-retardant rope. She whisked the rope off her utility belt (the superheroes' staple) and slung it toward the rock.

The camera focused on The Flame's anxious face as Raife caught the rope and looped it around the rock. The camera zoomed in on the rock as The Flame pulled the rope taut. She then swung herself to the other side of the pit and began to climb up. The white wolf barked and jumped at her legs, once effectively grasping an ankle between his paws. He'd probably get a piece of steak for that one.

The Flame hauled herself up the wall of the pit and onto the ground above. She heaved a sigh of relief, but alas, her safety was short-lived. Wild Man, a sixty-eight-year-old retired banker with a vested interest in the station and an unfulfilled childhood fantasy of being the next Clark Gable, awaited her. Wild Man's costume looked like an old bear suit with the head and arms cut out. It was so shabby in some places that if he hadn't been constantly kept in the shadows it would have appeared that Wild Man had mange.

Wild Man raced toward The Flame as far as the shadows would allow him to go and roared mightily. At least, as mightily as a two-pack-a-day cigarette habit would permit. "Back in the pit with you, Flame! Back to the snarling beast who waits to devour you!"

"Not this time, Wild Man. You caught me off guard before, but I'm ready for you now." She pulled out her immobilizer (a wax banana covered with foil) and aimed it at Wild Man. When she squeezed the immobilizer's trigger, it crumpled and banana began to ooze out of the foil.

Beryl gasped. That wasn't supposed to have happened! Raife must've used a real banana rather than a wax one. How was she going to improvise this? "You...you...you monster!" She glared at Wild Man as she tossed the banana aside. "The...acidic disseminator! You threw it on my immobilizer!"

Wild Man laughed harshly. "That I did! What will you do now?"

How should I know? Beryl thought. "The white wolf!" she cried, peering over into the pit.

Wild Man came closer to see what she was doing. As Wild Man leaned over the pit, The Flame pushed him in. She then placed her fists on her hips and said, "I'm sorry to do that to you, Wild Man, but you left me no choice." She then turned and ran.

As the camera zoomed in on Wild Man ranting and swearing revenge, Beryl slipped off her boots and pulled jeans and a sweatshirt on over her catsuit. She wiggled her feet into a pair of canvas sneakers as Raife undid her hair and removed her mask. Beryl hurried back over to a different set, this one made up to look like a den. It was where The Flame called home when she was her alter ego, Bess Keene.

In this shot, Bess was researching a string of related jewel thefts on her computer. "This has to be the work of The Gemstones," she muttered to her cat, Smoky. "Pearl, Ruby, Jade and Opal are at it again."

Raife did the voiceover as Beryl sat and held Smoky. She stroked the cat as she looked at the computer with fierce determination, lending credence to Raife's contention that The Flame would be forced to once again extinguish the plans of that "sticky-fingered foursome."

"Cut, people!" Joe called. "Good job. Good save, Beryl. Raife, what happened?"

As Raife tried to explain the gun blunder to Joe, Beryl walked off the set. She had to hurry and change, as today was an IRS day. She nearly ran headlong into Terry, who was bent over wiping some banana off his shoe.

"Mr. Goodson? What--?" Beryl shook her head uncomprehendingly.

"Oh, this. Would you ask The Flame not to toss her immobilizer at me next time?"

"Did I? Oh, Terry, I didn't mean to. I'm sorry." Her words were contradicted by the giggle that finally escaped her.

"Uh-huh. I came by to bring you some information about the camping trip." He handed her a manila envelope. "Have you had breakfast yet?"

"No. I'll grab a doughnut or something on my way out."

"Don't do that. Have breakfast with me."

"I can't this morning. I have to be at work at the IRS in about half an hour."

"Oh, well. Maybe we can do breakfast some other time."

Terry winked as he left, leaving Beryl with no doubt as to his insinuation. The thought gave her the shivers...the good kind.

"Hey, hey," Raife said, from behind Beryl. "Who's the hottie with the sexual innuendo?"

"It's Duncan's teacher, Terry Goodson," Beryl said, reluctantly turning away from Terry's retreating form. "I'm helping out with a project this weekend." She held up the envelope for verification.

Raife raised his dark brows. "What type of project? Show and tell?"

"It's a camping trip!"

"Even better."

"Raife!"

He laughed. "Don't 'Raife' me! I say, go for it, girl."

"It's not like that."

"Yet."

"I have the boys to think about."

"So? Don't you still have yourself to think about, too?"

"Not ahead of them, no."

"You don't have to put yourself ahead of them. Just don't

leave yourself completely out." Raife tsked. "You'll come around, baby girl."

Beryl shook her head. "I've got all the relationships I can handle in my life right now. Two guys are more than enough."

"Yes, but what you have now are two little boys--not two men. Big difference." He wagged a finger. "Big difference."

"I don't know about that," Beryl said with a laugh.

"I do." Raife gave her a fraternal hug. "Besides, you don't have to have a relationship to have the man, honey."

"I do."

"I know it. What am I gonna do with you?"

"Fix my hair and makeup so I can go to my other job?"

"You got it."

B eryl was on her way out the door when she ran into Bob March, almost literally. His bulky frame filled the doorway, and it was obvious he wasn't moving.

"What's the hurry, girl?" he said, his voice ringing out jovially.

"I've got to get to my other job, Mr. March."

"That young man you were talking to earlier...he looked familiar. What's his name?"

"Terry Goodson. I believe you did his uncle's estate?"

"Yeah...yeah, that's right. I did." His gray eyes narrowed. "How'd you know? Are you two friends?"

"He's Duncan's teacher."

He nodded, his fluffy white hair bobbing like cotton candy. "How are the tots? Adjusting okay?"

"They seem to be." She flipped her wrist over, pointedly looking at her watch. "I really have to run. Nice seeing you."

"You, too, Beryl." He shoved a tan Stetson onto his head, making Beryl feel more like she was in Texas than Tennessee, and gallantly stepped aside.

Beryl could feel his eyes on her as she strode to her car. She turned and waved to him. He nodded, turned and disappeared down the hall.

Beryl arrived at work on a wing and a prayer but still fifteen minutes late. She hurried into her office hoping the Dragon Lady hadn't noticed.

She still had Bob March on her mind, and she pulled Terry's file from her outbox. For once, she was thankful that her secretary was as slow as a turtle trudging through a puddle of molasses.

Beryl opened the file and flipped through the pages until she came to the final accounting. She took a legal pad from her top drawer and quickly jotted down the expenses and amounts. Many of the expenses did seem extreme, but then, Beryl hadn't known Terry's uncle. Perhaps the man had had expensive tastes or had left explicit instructions in his will. Yet, Raife's words about Bob March came back to her. "What does surprise me is that you've not heard rumors about him before this... I figured surely he wouldn't screw you...or your family. He knows you."

The brisk knock that Beryl had been dreading sounded at the door. It was Nancy's "you're-in-trouble-and-I-can't-wait-to-tell-you-about-it-knock." It was the only time Beryl ever saw something resembling a sincere smile on Nancy's face.

She closed Terry's file, put it in the outbox, and flipped over the legal pad as Nancy sauntered into her office. Unable to conceal the smug little smile, Nancy shut the door behind her.

"A wee bit late this morning, weren't we, Beryl? Does nine o'clock not suit you anymore?"

"I'm sorry. I...ran into some difficulties this morning."

"Hmmm. Odd that you would run into difficulties on one of the three mornings you work here."

Beryl refused to give Nancy the satisfaction of clinching her fists, so she curled her toes.

"One wonders," Nancy continued, "how often you would run into difficulties if you were working here full time."

"I'll work through lunch to make up the fifteen minutes I was late this morning."

"Suit yourself. I was simply making sure you're not having...difficulties...that you cannot handle on your own."

"I can handle my difficulties fine, thank you."

"Yes, well, if you need to rework your schedule, take a bit of time off...what have you, by all means, let me know and we'll discuss it."

"Thank you."

Beryl's phone rang. She welcomed the interruption until Raife's voice greeted her. He was apologizing and trying to explain about the banana incident. He'd apparently got a chewing out from Joe over it.

"It's okay," Beryl said, willing her eyes away from Nancy, who continued to stand in her office. "It's...it's all right. We'll talk about this later, okay?"

Nancy cleared her throat noisily, forcing Beryl to look up at her.

"I'll go now so you can finish your personal call," Nancy stage whispered.

Beryl slumped in her chair. Fifteen minutes late and a personal phone call. All she needed was one more strike today. And if Nancy Carruthers knew she'd met Terry Goodson for lunch yesterday, that would be it.

Beryl quickly ended her call from Raife by telling him she was really swamped with things she had to get done before lunch. It wasn't really a lie, and he felt too guilty about the banana incident for Beryl to make him feel worse by letting him know Nancy had been in the room when he'd called.

She sighed, picked up her empty coffee cup, and was debating whether or not she dared to go for a refill when a timid knock came at the door.

Clark. Had to be.

She sat the cup back down and massaged her right temple where a dull ache was beginning to spread. "Come on in."

"Hi," Clark said, bumping his knee on the door as he navigated his wiry frame into the room. "You...you sound...tired or something." He closed the door back behind him. "You... um...okay?"

"Fine." Beryl smiled stiffly. "How can I help you this morning, Clark?"

"Oh...um...actually, you...you already have." He pushed glasses too large for his small face back upon the bridge of his nose. "Y-yesterday. I came to say thanks.... I appreciate your taking my audits for me while I was out. I had a terrible allergy attack." As if to underscore this, he sneezed.

Beryl saw it coming in time to quickly scoot herself away from the desk, but watching the spray envelope everything on the desk made her decision about going for coffee much easier. Maybe tomorrow after her cup had been scalded.

"No problem," she said.

"Well, I...I want you to know I'm very grateful. You had to take on my work when you have plenty of your own to do...."

"No problem," Beryl repeated. "I'm glad you're feeling

better."

"Can I make it up to you by buying you lunch?"

"I can't today, Clark. I was late this morning, so I'll need to grab a sandwich and eat at my desk."

"Oh...okay. Another time then?"

"Sure." Beryl looked at Clark expectantly, waiting for him to get up and leave. When he didn't, she became concerned that he was going to try to pin her down on that "sure," and make a date. She quickly grabbed a file from her inbox and looked at her watch. "If you'll excuse me, Clark, I have an audit in half an hour and I need to review this file."

"Of course...of course." Clark stood abruptly, upsetting the chair when he did so. It toppled backward and hit the bookshelf knocking over half a dozen reference manuals and causing Beryl's African violet to crash to the floor.

"Oh! I'm...I'm so sorry...so...sorry." As he scrambled around trying to put things back in order, he stepped on the violet. He spun around to assess the damage to the flower and his skinny butt hit the bookshelf knocking off three more books.

Between Clark's apologies and professions of regret, Beryl was able to work in enough words edgewise to assure him that everything was fine and that she'd clean up the mess herself. She ushered him out the door. As soon as she closed the door behind him, she leaned against it, closed her eyes and sighed heavily. Her mother had given her that violet on her first day here. Now it was ruined. She glumly scooped it up and deposited it into the trashcan. As she re-shelved the books and righted the chair, Beryl was afraid to wonder what would happen next in this delightful day.

Fortunately, the rest of Beryl's work day passed without incident. But then there was the remainder of the day to get through.

From inside the van, Beryl searched for Duncan in the throng of children pouring from the school. Though she couldn't spot Duncan, her eyes had no problem detecting Terry Goodson. She tried to tell herself that it was because he was a good two feet taller than the crowd surrounding him, but the truth was he would've stood out in any crowd. The day was a great deal sunnier than Beryl's disposition, and that sunlight played upon

Terry's sandy hair highlighting strands of gold. He wore black slacks today and a bright red polo shirt. Suddenly, he looked her way, smiled broadly, and called, "Hi!"

Beryl returned his smile, wet her lips, sat up a bit straighter, and hoped that her makeup had withstood her rotten day.

"Hi!"

Though Beryl had opened her mouth to speak, she'd not yet done so. She turned to see an attractive woman in a navy jogging suit sashay by the van toward Terry. He'd been speaking to her. He hadn't even noticed Beryl. And if he had, it hadn't made enough difference to him to come over and say "hello" or to yell out such an enthusiastic "Hi!"

Beryl started as the door opened.

"Hey, Aunt B," Duncan said. "Somethin' wrong?"

"No...no, sweetie, of course not." She nodded toward Miss-Bouncy-Big-Hair. "Who's she?"

"She's Miss Robbins, the gym teacher."

"Hmmm."

Beryl watched the cordial exchange between Miss Robbins and Terry with some interest. She shook off her pique as The Flame's persona wormed its way into her thoughts.

What a poor misguided woman this Miss Robbins must be. How could a mere mortal hope to compete with The Flame for a man's attentions? Not that The Flame wanted this man's attentions. This man's attentions were the last thing either The Flame or Beryl Madison needed or wanted right now...but if they did, they'd have them. Signed, sealed and delivered. Sure, they would.

As Beryl followed the train of vehicles out of the parking lot, she caught a glimpse of Terry waving at them. Duncan responded with an excited wave. Beryl pretended she didn't see him...or The Bimbo either, for that matter.

They could use a new character for the show. Beryl could see it now:

The Bimbo--her modus operandi would be knocking over cosmetic counters and clothing stores. Estee Lauder, Clarins, Maybelline, Lancome, Revlon-- The Bimbo has no preference. Where there are bright and glitzy colors, The Bimbo will make an appearance. Where there's a free sample to be given, The Bimbo will want her fair share...and then some. Clearance sale? You'll find The Bimbo lying on the fitting room floor squeezing into a pair of jeans two sizes too small. And when she squirms to her feet, it'll be to dash--not to the checkout register--but to the exit.

Not bad. Beryl would have to talk with Joe about it. She put The Bimbo out of her mind, feeling only a twinge of guilt over going to two different Clarins' counters to receive a free sample of foundation this past weekend. Perhaps there was a little "Bimbo" buried deep down in all of us.

After picking up Dominic from the day care center, Beryl hustled the boys over to the grocery store. A friend of Dad's was staying with him for a few hours this evening in order to give Molly a break, and she was coming by to see Beryl and the boys. It was rare that Molly had a little time to relax, and Beryl wanted to treat her to a nice supper. When Beryl relayed this information to the boys, they were surprised to find themselves in front of a grocery store rather than a take-out restaurant.

"I know I'm not the world's greatest cook...yet," Beryl said, "but I want Grandma to have a home cooked meal that she didn't have to make tonight. Surely I can find something in here that isn't too difficult to make."

"Whatever you say, Aunt B," Duncan said.

"Don't you guys have any faith in me whatsoever?"

"I do," Dominic proclaimed. "I have face."

"Me, too," Duncan said, looking down at his backpack and tracing the design with a forefinger. "I guess I just...I still miss Mom sometimes. She...could cook real good, you know...make all my favorite things...."

Beryl unbuckled her seat belt and slid over to envelop Duncan in a hug. "I know, sweetie, I know. And I'm trying...."

"I miss Mommy, too," Dominic said.

Beryl leaned over the seat and stroked Dominic's hair. "I know, baby."

"I not a baby. I a big boy."

"I know that, too, sweetie." Beryl felt like dropping her head into her hands and sobbing. Maybe later. She couldn't allow herself the luxury of wallowing in self-pity right now. "Come on, guys. Let's go see if we can gather up the ingredients to make Grandma a great meal."

While not a complete success, dinner was not a complete flop either. The steak was tender and juicy, not completely done in the center, but several bites on the fringes were palatable. The baked potatoes weren't too hard, the homemade biscuits were bricks that the neighbor's dog chose to bury rather than eat, and, of course, the cake (from the grocery's bakery) was absolute perfection. Dominic was still trying to figure out whose birthday it was when he went to bed.

When at last both boys were asleep in their beds, Molly and Beryl sank down on opposite ends of the couch with tired sighs.

"So, how are you, baby?"

"How are you, Mama?"

They'd spoken at once and laughed at themselves.

"You first," Beryl said.

Molly smiled. "I'm fine."

"Are you?"

"Yeah," Molly said with a shrug. "I miss Ralph sometimes. Occasionally, I even think it might've been easier for me if he'd just died. At least then I wouldn't have to watch him die a little each day." She shrugged again. "Then I feel guilty as hell." She gave Beryl a wan smile.

"You're just human, Mama."

"I know. And sometimes I see glimpses of my sweet old Ralph, and I'm glad he's still with me."

"You know," Beryl said, lowering her voice to a whisper, "sometimes I'm still angry with August and Ron...especially August."

Molly nodded. "The boys are a big responsibility."

"It's not that." She lowered her eyes. "I'd lived my whole life in August's shadow. She was the pretty one, the feminine one, the domestic one, the perfect one. Then I went off to college, glad to escape the constant comparisons...sure that I'd carve out my own niche in this world and never have to be compared to August again." She looked back up at her mother. "Now, here again, I'm being compared to her--and found wanting--every day of my life."

Molly took her hands. "Oh, baby, you're not."

"I am, Mama. I am." Then Beryl succumbed to the tears that had been threatening all day.

Molly squeezed her daughter's hands. "Listen to me," she said. "You've never been compared to anyone, and you aren't being compared now...unless you're doing it to yourself."

Beryl sniffled. "But--"

"But nothing. You and August are...were...two wonderfully

different people. Her strengths were your weaknesses, but that worked both ways. She envied you the things you could do that she couldn't."

"Like what?"

"Like being independent and strong." Molly released one of Beryl's hands long enough to wipe away a tear of her own. "I never told you this because I figured you knew--" She looked down at their clasped hands. "But when August and Ron made out their will, August told me she wanted the boys to live with you if anything ever happened to her and Ron because she wanted them to grow up knowing your strength." She smiled. "She wanted them to be free thinkers... just like you. 'I don't want anybody pushing my babies around,' she said."

"She did? She said that...about me?"

Molly nodded. "She sure did. She knew I'd help you if and when you needed me, but she also knew that you'd take good care of her children. And you do."

Beryl smiled. "Thanks, Mama."

"Just don't ever go comparing yourself to anyone ever again. You're incomparable, Beryl Madison. Remember that."

4

When Terry stepped onto Beryl's porch on Thursday evening, he could see through the screen door that Beryl and Dominic were looking at some sort of books while Raife and Duncan sat in front of the coffee table. It seemed Raife was teaching Duncan to draw. Terry hesitantly tapped on the door.

"I'm sorry," he said, when Beryl opened the door. "I didn't intend to interrupt. I just wanted to go over some last-minute details about the camping trip."

"Okay. Come on in." Beryl held the door open and Terry stepped inside.

He surveyed the room. It was comfortable and homey. While not cluttered, it had a definite lived-in, family feel. The sofa was covered in a dark-hued plaid material that Terry assumed would kindly hide spills and crumbs. A navy armchair took its color from one of the stripes in the sofa and was placed near an overstuffed bookshelf.

He nodded toward the chair. "I'll bet that's your favorite spot in the house."

"You're right," Beryl said, tugging at the hem of her pink tank top.

"Hi, Mr. Goodson," Duncan said.

Dominic shyly hid behind one of Beryl's shapely legs, drawing Terry's attention to Beryl's snug white shorts...not that his attention had needed much prompting.

"Nice to see you again," Raife commented with a nod. "Excuse me. I need to check on dinner."

So this was as intimate a scene as Terry had first thought. He continued to peruse the room. Sitting atop a table near a window was a vase filled with yellow roses.

He nodded. "Beautiful."

Raife returned to the living room.

"You have good taste," Terry told him. In flowers, yes, but especially, in women.

Raife wrinkled his nose in distaste. "When I send roses, I send white ones. *Tres chic.*"

"But the yellow ones smell divine," Beryl said.

Frowning, Terry turned to Beryl.

"Those are from Clark Samuels," she explained, "to thank me for taking care of his audits on Tuesday."

"Yeah...he's got it bad for Aunt B."

"Oh, Duncan, he does not."

Raife spread his hands. "Oh, yes, he does! Duncan's a guy--he knows these things."

"Yeah! I know these things!" Duncan beamed, delighted to be a guy who knows things.

"Whatever," Beryl said, waving her hand. "Why don't you three go bond in the kitchen? Dominic and I will stay out here and finish the coloring books."

"Finish them?" Terry asked.

"Yes. Raife and Duncan do the drawing, and Dominic and I do the binding."

"Hey, let's see." Terry picked up one of the completed coloring books and thumbed through it. "These are great! Duncan, what did you draw?"

"Well, Raife draws Aunt B, Wild Man, and the animals and stuff. I do the trees, rocks, flowers and things."

"Really?" Terry asked. "That's fantastic. Maybe you could talk about it to the class one day."

"Sure," Duncan said, with a self-deprecating shrug that belied the pride sparkling in his dark eyes.

Raife put a hand on Terry's shoulder. "Why don't you take that one with you? You haven't lived until you've painted The Flame." He waggled his eyebrows.

Beryl snapped her fingers and pointed to the kitchen. "Stop misbehaving and get in there and finish dinner, Raife. You can help too, Mr. Goodson. You're here--you might as well eat."

"Oh, but I--"

"No 'buts'. You three get in the kitchen...and I want to hear work being done not jokes being made. Dominic and I have to finish up these books." Beryl looked down at the cherub still fastened to her leg. "Don't we, dumpling?"

He nodded.

Terry bent down to eye-level with Dominic. "I hear you're going camping with us tomorrow."

Dominic nodded.

"I'm glad. We're going to have a lot of fun." He lowered his voice to a whisper. "It's fun being a big boy, isn't it?"

Dominic merely nodded again, but this time he rewarded Terry with a broad grin.

Within minutes, dinner was ready and everyone was seated around the oval oak table in the dining room.

"This is nice," Terry said, biting into a croissant filled with chunks of ham and cheddar. "I usually either eat out or stand over the sink and eat a sandwich." He chuckled. "I don't even have a kitchen table...only two bar stools pushed up against the island in the middle of the kitchen. Ah, well...such is the life of a bachelor, eh, Raife?"

Raife smiled tightly and reached for another helping of macaroni salad.

"What does your kitchen look like?" Terry asked.

"Just a kitchen."

"Aw, come on," Terry persisted. "Tell us what your 'dining area' looks like, Raife. It can't be as bad as mine."

Beryl smiled. "Go ahead, Raife. Tell him about your kitchen and dining room."

"Beryl, I--"

"If you don't, I will," she said, nearly bubbling with laughter.

"All right. I, too, have an island in my kitchen with stools on either side."

Terry laughed and nodded.

"My pots hang on a copper rack suspended from the ceiling over the island, and the top of the island is made of butcher's block so I can use it to chop vegetables," Raife continued. He waved the spoon from the macaroni salad back and forth. "But never meat. I have a glass cutting board for meats so that afterward I can pop it

GAYLE TRENT

in the dishwasher and sanitize it. As for my dining room suite, I have a cherry table, hutch and buffet that were made back in the '30's. I got them at an estate sale for a song. They're exquisite."

"Hmmm. Sounds super." Terry had a feeling his smile was a bit weak now. "I'd ask you to let me know the next time you hear about one of those estate sales, but I'd be a hypocrite if I did. I'll get furniture like that when I'm ready to settle down...many, many years from now."

"Maybe you should simply save what you have," Beryl said. "By then, perhaps they'll be antiques."

"You're right." He raised his iced tea glass in a mock toast.

"Mr. Goodson," Duncan asked, "would it be cheating for you to help me with my homework...you know, since you're here and all?"

"No, it wouldn't be cheating. I help kids with their homework every day." He pushed back away from the table. "Let's go back in here in the living room. Beryl, Raife, thank you for dinner."

"You're welcome."

They said it in unison and then smiled at each other. Raife winked at Beryl.

To Terry it was obvious they were a couple who knew each other well and were comfortable with each other. Very comfortable. Like best friends. He was glad he'd realized Raife was gay.

"He thinks we're an item, you know," Raife said as soon as Terry, Duncan and Dominic (who promised to be quiet and "jus' wash") was out of earshot.

"So? I don't care what he thinks."

"Don't you?" Raife arched a brow in an arrogant, I-know-better expression.

"No, I don't." Beryl stood and began stacking the dishes. As she reached for Raife's plate, she slid her free hand down his arm feeling the hard muscle beneath the brown silk shirt. "I could do much worse than you."

"I know." Laughing, he grabbed her hand and kissed her palm. "But you know you're not my type, baby girl. And I know I'm not your type either. You're just trying to land a man who can cook for these kids."

38

She sighed. "Oh, well, you can't blame a girl for trying." She picked up the plates and moved them to the counter.

Raife looked at his watch. "I have to run. After the show tomorrow, I'll French braid your hair for the camping trip if you'd like."

"I'd love it. Thanks."

He kissed her cheek. "You be careful, baby girl...because I'll let you in on something. Clark Samuels isn't the only one who has it bad for you."

Beryl scoffed. "If you mean Terry Goodson, forget it. I think he is the quintessential Peter Pan, and the last thing the boys need is someone who's gonna run out on them and fly off to Neverland."

Raife shrugged. "I'm just telling you, guys know these things. I doubt he went to every chaperone's house to go over last minute camping details. Besides, what is there to go over? You try to keep a group of rowdy boys from killing you and each other for two days." He smoothed her hair. "Be careful."

"You think he's a heartbreaker, don't you?"

"He'd better not break yours." He jerked his head in the direction of the living room. "Or theirs. See you in the morning."

Beryl loaded the dishwasher, thinking as she did so, that Raife had nothing to worry about. She certainly wouldn't give Terry Goodson a chance to break her heart, much less the boys'.

"Beryl?"

She started at the sound of Terry's husky voice and nearly dropped a glass. "Y-yeah?"

"Duncan has finished his homework, and I wondered if we could go over a few things about the camping trip now."

"Of course." She placed the glass in the dishwasher and wiped her hands down the back of her shorts. Terry's sky blue eyes seemed to drill all the way through her. "I--" She pulled out a chair. "Have a seat."

Terry moved slowly toward the table and gestured for her to sit in the chair she'd pulled out. She did so and Terry slid the chair up to the table, his fingers grazing her bare shoulders.

Terry took the chair adjacent to hers. "You and Raife have known each other for quite a while, haven't you?"

"Is it that obvious?"

"Mmm-hmm." He stroked his chin with his thumb and index finger. "He your best friend?"

"Mmm-hmm. Why?"

He shrugged. "When I came in, I thought you guys made a fairly intimate, familial scene."

"Thanks. I think it's important to Duncan and Dominic to have a man in their lives." She narrowed her eyes. "Why do I sense some type of 'but' in what you're saying?"

"Raife is gay, isn't he?"

"Yes, so? He's our friend."

"He's safe."

"I beg your pardon."

"He's a male influence in the boy's life that you don't have to be afraid of."

"He's a man that I don't have to be afraid will disappear on them, if that's what you mean." Beryl placed her forearms on the table and leaned forward. "What does any of this have to do with the camping trip?"

"Not a thing. I just--" Terry spread his hands.

"You just what, Dr. Freud? You're just still trying to analyze me? If so, then give it up already. I'll see a shrink on my own if and when I need one."

"Fine. Sorry I stepped on your toes." With a flick of his wrist, Terry changed the subject. "We have to be at the campground by four-thirty tomorrow afternoon. Is that a problem for you?"

"No." Beryl wet her lips. "Where are the boys?"

"Duncan took Dominic upstairs to his room to watch the baseball game on TV."

"Okay."

"Duncan wants to go up with the rest of the boys in the bus," Terry said.

Beryl nodded. "I know. I'm to bring Dominic in the Camaro. However, I refuse to dress like one of Beyonce's dancers or be called B.M."

"I won't ask."

"Please don't."

They discussed a few more minor details about the camping trip, and then Beryl looked up at the clock.

"I'd better go up and check on the boys. They need to start getting ready for bed."

"I need to be going, too."

They stood, and Beryl nearly tripped over her chair in her haste to get away from the table. Terry's strong arms reached out and caught her.

"You okay?" he asked.

"Fine."

Neither moved away from the near-embrace, and as Beryl looked up into his eyes, Terry lowered his lips to hers. The next thing Beryl knew, her hands were in his hair pulling his mouth against hers, her passion matching the fever pitch of his own. He crushed her body to his.

You be careful, baby girl.

Raife's warning echoed in Beryl's head. She willed herself to extricate her hands from Terry's hair, place them against his chest and lightly push him away. She gave him a falsely bright smile as she combed his hair back down with her fingers.

"Next time we do this, there have to be more people, and we have to have a bottle," Beryl said.

"What?" Terry asked, shaking his head as if to clear it.

"Spin the bottle! I guess all that talk about camping kinda got to us."

He nodded slowly. "Yeah."

"Let me walk you out." She led the way to the front door hoping her brisk steps hid the trembling of her legs. She opened the door with a flourish. "See you at camp tomorrow!"

"Yeah. See you tomorrow. Say goodnight to the boys for me."

"I'll do that." Beryl still smiled as she closed the screen door and even as she shut the main door. Then she groaned, put her head in her hands and sank to the floor.

Later Terry sat in his apartment watching a television that was sitting on the floor. He picked at the frayed arm of the sofa that had been given to him by Aunt Louise after Uncle Jack had died. The sofa had been in Uncle Jack's "den." Translation - basement room that Uncle Jack never got around to finishing. In fact, it had had a dirt floor and consisted only of the sofa Terry was now sitting on and an old, black-and-white television set. It was, Terry supposed, very much like his living room except that he had wall-to-wall carpeting and a color TV. The so-called den was where Uncle Jack had gone whenever he'd wanted to hide for a little while.

There was a burst of canned laughter on the television show, and Terry looked up to see what was funny. Nothing.

Was this where *he* came to hide? Maybe he was hiding, if you wanted to call it that. But to Terry, he was simply maintaining his freedom…his independence. Nobody would ever take that away. Not even Beryl Madison.

He sighed and ran his hands over his face. Now, where had that come from? From that kiss, that's where. He was merely lusting after the woman and worrying that it was something else. It hadn't ever been anything serious with anyone else, so why would Beryl be any different?

It would be nice to spend a little time with Beryl…have a little fun…but he didn't want to get into a sticky situation with one of his students' guardians. And it certainly could be sticky. Beryl just might be looking for a dad for the boys.

They were great boys, but Terry was most definitely not ready or willing to be a father at this point in his life. So far, he'd avoided belonging to anybody…avoided having anybody other than himself be the crux of his existence…and nobody belonged to him. He had no real responsibility to anyone except himself…and he liked it that way.

He wondered if Beryl had felt the same way about her single life before her circumstances changed. She was devoted to the boys— anyone could see that—and she was doing an excellent job with them. Still, she'd had no choice about whether or not she was going to belong to Duncan and Dominic, and vice versa. Or did she? There was always a choice, he guessed.

Since Uncle Jack's death, Aunt Louise had become a pale shadow of the woman she'd once been. Her world…heart…personality…entire life had crumbled upon losing Uncle Jack. Terry didn't want anyone to ever have that kind of power over him.

Yet, he couldn't take his mind off how wonderful it had felt to be in Beryl's arms…holding her…kissing her. He'd wanted to make love to her so badly. Still did.

The phone rang, jerking him out of his reverie.

"Hello?"

"Hi, Terry. Pam Robbins here. Have you been running? You sound out of breath."

"What's up?"

"Can you do bus duty for me in the morning? I know that'll put you there both early and late since you have afternoon bus duty of your own, but...."

"Sure, Pam. No problem."

"Can I make you dinner next week to make it up to you?"

"Um...yeah, sure."

"What day?"

"I don't know. Look, I have to go right now. I'll talk to you later."

"Well, bye."

Pam rang off in a huff, and Terry wondered if he'd blown his chances with her. Probably not. She'd made it a point to see him every day since school started. Here she was practically offering that luscious body of hers to him on a silver platter...and all he could think about was Beryl Madison.

There's always a choice, he reminded himself.

But sometimes your heart makes it for you, a little voice inside taunted.

5

Camp Wannameyer fell far short of Beryl's expectations. In her opinion, it should've been called Camp Wannabe. Rather than the picturesque cabins overlooking the sparkling lake she'd imagined, there were so many little shacks in a field, and in the center of the field there was a murky, greenish pond. A couple of canoes lay against the bank, their white paint peeling pitifully and adding to the forlorn ambience of the "lake."

Beryl heaved the gearshift to park, cut the engine, folded her arms across the steering wheel and gazed out at the wonderland where she'd be spending the next two days. *I'm doing this for Duncan. I'm doing this for Duncan.*

"Aunt B," Dominic said.

She turned and gave the little urchin a wan smile.

"I gotta pee."

Beryl's eyes widened and she hurriedly fumbled to unfasten her seatbelt. "Just hold on," she said. "I'll come around and get you and we'll find a bathroom."

Potty training was a toughie. Dominic had been doing well until his parents "had to go away for a while," and then he'd regressed. Beryl thought she'd probably thrown away and replaced hundreds-- or at least, tens--of pairs of underwear in the past six months. She could deal with the wet ones, but she didn't have the stomach for cleaning the really soiled ones.

She raced around to the passenger side of the car and began unfastening Dominic. "We're gonna make it, big guy. We're gonna make it."

"We better hurry," he warned.

"Hello," Terry said, as he got off the bus and strode over to Beryl's car. "Hey there, Dominic. Your cabin is--"

Beryl hoisted Dominic onto her hip. "In a minute. We need to find a bathroom. Quick!"

"Oh," Terry said with grin. "There's a couple outhouses out behind the cabins."

"Outhouses?!" Beryl couldn't have looked more horrified if Terry had told her he was going to set her hair on fire.

"Yeah," he said. "That's not a problem, is it?"

"You'd better believe it's a problem! I'm not using an outdoor toilet, and this baby isn't either!"

"I not a baby! I a big guy!"

"I know, I know," Beryl said. "But you're not using a snake-infested outhouse. We'll just get in the car and go to that restaurant that I spotted about half a mile back."

Terry threw back his head and laughed. "I'm only joking. Each cabin has its own facilities."

Beryl closed her eyes as she felt the warm saturation of her shirt. "Thanks, Mr. Goodson. Thanks a lot." She stomped to the rear of the car and opened the trunk. There, she slung two duffel bags over her shoulder and grabbed a shopping bag and a package of unopened toddler briefs. She slammed down the lid of the trunk and glared at Terry. "Which one's ours?"

"What are you mad at me for? It was only a joke."

"Which cabin is ours? Dominic and I need to change now."

"Oh." Terry winced. "Sorry."

Tired of waiting for Terry to assign her and Dominic a cabin, Beryl stormed off in the direction of the nasty, tiny, so-called dwellings. She supposed it beat sleeping in a refrigerator box...though it wasn't much bigger. If these things had their own bathrooms, the commode must be situated either at the foot of the bed or in the closet. She had no idea how a bathtub could be crammed in any two of these hovels put together.

"Wait," Terry called. "You'll need the key."

She stopped and waited for him to get beside her. He held out the key.

"Hand it to Dominic please. I have my hands full."

Terry gave Dominic the key. "Are you going to pout at me all weekend?" he asked Beryl.

"Probably." She nodded in the direction of the cabins. "Which one, slumlord?"

"Hey, we could've pitched tents. I think these cabins are pretty nice. At least the boys will get to sleep in beds and have a roof over their heads…. And so will we."

"Which one?"

"Number Fifteen. Now, if you'll excuse me, your majesty, I need to help the boys get settled in."

Beryl quickly located Cabin 15, even though the five dangled upside down, and sat Dominic on the rickety porch. She took the key from him and unlocked the door. For once, he didn't argue for her to "Lemmee! Lemmee do it!" Holding her breath, she stepped inside. A restraining hand kept Dominic on the porch until Beryl could flip on a light and see what they were up against.

"Huh," Beryl said, dropping her hand.

"Whatizit?" Dominic asked.

"Come on in, dumpling. It's…it's actually okay." She sat the duffel bags on the floor and took another look around the room.

There were two twin-sized beds at the back of the room, each covered with a red chenille bedspread which appeared to be in good condition… clean… beginning to wear thin, but no holes were apparent. There was a small, round table beside each bed and a reading lamp mounted onto the wall above each bed. In the center of the room, a blue and red braided rug had been placed across the hardwood floor. On the rug sat two wooden rocking chairs and a padded wooden bench.

"This isn't bad at all," Beryl said.

"I like it," Dominic said.

"So do I. Now let's get on some dry clothes."

"'Kay."

Beryl retrieved the package of toddler briefs. "What do you want to go with this time?" she asked. "Pooh and the balloons or Eeyore and his thistles?"

"Eeyore."

"Yeah." Beryl ripped open the package. "I've always liked him, too." She put the briefs on one of the beds, opened her duffel bag and took out a washcloth. "We need to wash up a little bit, don't we?"

"Uh-huh." Dominic wrinkled his nose. "We snink, don't we,

Aunt B?"

"We sure do." She smiled and kissed the top of his head. "Whoa!" she said, stepping into the bathroom.

Dominic came running. "Whatizit?"

"This isn't bad, either! You can tell the fixtures are old--look at that claw foot tub--but they're clean."

"They clean?"

"Yes, dumpling, they're clean." She turned the hot water on and waited for it to get warm enough to wash Dominic. "Look, they even have soap." She unwrapped the tiny bar of soap and lathered up the washcloth. "After we both get bathed and changed, I'm going to make pies to take to the cookout."

"You gonna make pies?"

"I sure am. Won't Duncan be surprised?"

"Yeah." Dominic nodded. "And me, too."

The aroma of grilling hotdogs and hamburgers greeted Beryl and Dominic as they stepped out of their cabin and headed toward the middle of the field. Beryl had made four strawberry pies. She was carrying three, and Dominic was proudly carrying the other. At least, she could contribute something to the cookout.

August would probably have supplied each camper with his own individual chocolate mousse served in a plastic champagne glass with a perfect little dollop of whipped cream and an orange slice on the side of the glass (*for decoration only, mind you. Now, for adults we would put a cherry on top, of course, but that would never do for children. What if one of the little darlings got choked? Not only would it be horrifying, but we could open ourselves up for a lawsuit.*). At times, Beryl could image August's actions and reactions as if she were right in front of her. Practical and domestic, that was August.

August would never have settled for graham cracker crusts, chopped strawberries and pre-made strawberry pie filling to quickly throw together four strawberry pies. Oh, no. August would've taken great pains to make a perfect dessert...and she would've wanted everyone to know that she had taken great pains, and had everyone not said that the dessert was indeed perfect, they would've found themselves on her blacklist for who knows how long.

I miss you so bad, August.

Beryl looked down at the pie on top of the stack she carried. She had hurriedly spread whipped topping on top of the pies with the knife she'd used to chop the strawberries because she'd forgotten to bring a spatula. Thus, the now pinkish whipped topping looked as if it'd had been slung onto the pies with a butcher's knife--because it had been. And, thus, the same knife was going to have to be used to serve the pie…which meant that the pie would be slopped onto the plates in a strawberry-graham cracker-whipped topping gob that would look about as appetizing as that murky pond out there. Wouldn't August be proud of Beryl's mothering abilities?

Yes, she would have.

It was as if Beryl could hear Molly dishing out a reprimand.

Being well aware of your cooking limitations, August would have been touched that you cared enough to make pies for her sons and their friends.

"Hey!" one of the boys yelled when he saw Beryl and Dominic approaching. "They've got pies!"

"Pies?" Duncan hurried forward, ostensibly to help Beryl, but really to check out the pies. "Where'd ya get these, Aunt B?"

"She made 'em," Dominic said. "I washed her."

"Really?" Duncan asked. "You made 'em?"

"Yes, Duncan, I really did. Don't you believe Dominic? He did watch me, you know."

Dominic gave his brother a solemn nod.

"It was easy," Beryl continued. "I hope they'll be all right."

"Me, too," Duncan said.

Beryl rolled her eyes heavenward. *I'm doing the best I can.*

"Need some help with those?" Terry called.

"Please," Beryl said.

"Not me," Dominic said. "I big."

"I know…but I think your aunt could use a hand." Terry took the pies and placed them on one of the picnic tables. "Thanks for bringing these. I was afraid we wouldn't have any dessert." He returned to the grill.

"Duncan, can you watch Dominic for a minute? I'll see if Mr. Goodson needs any help."

"Aw, Aunt B."

Beryl put her hands on her hips and was about to remind Duncan that the only way anyone got to come on this camping trip was because Dominic could come, when Terry came over, picked

Dominic up and sat him on his shoulders.

"Want to help me fix the burgers, big guy?" Terry asked.

"Yeah!"

"Are you sure that's safe?" Beryl asked, following them back over to the grill. "I mean, with all that smoke billowing around, and if you should drop him--"

"I won't drop him, and I won't let him be overcome by smoke inhalation," Terry said. "The burgers are done. I just have to put them on a plate…. I'm sure Dominic will be fine for that long."

"I'm sorry."

"You must not have a very high opinion of me, Ms. Madison."

Beryl sighed. "Look, I'm sorry about this afternoon. I was frustrated, that's all."

Terry shrugged and ignored her apology. "Everybody grab a plate and let's eat! Grillers first!" He lifted Dominic back down onto the ground. "That means us."

Within forty-five minutes, all the food was gone, even the ugly strawberry pies. And ugly though they were, even Beryl had to admit they were pretty tasty. She was pleased to see Terry having a second piece…or glob, as her assumption about the knife not doing an adequate job as a pie server had been correct.

"May I have your attention please?" Terry asked, as dinner was slowly, noisily coming to an end. "We have a little time yet before it's going to be dark enough for the stars to come out and allow us to study some of the constellations, so what would you guys like to do?"

"Ghost stories!" was the unanimous response.

"All right," Terry said. "How about we let the chaperones go first, and then you guys can see how lame our stories are and scare us half to death with your own stories?"

Beryl slapped at a mosquito that was trying to snack on her forearm. She supposed she could tell a story about that bloodthirsty little parasite. Maybe it had bitten someone with a chronic blood disease and was then going around infecting an entire village.

Nah. Too much like a bad movie of the week…or an episode of *The Flame*. She mentally added that to the plot lines she wanted to discuss with Joe--although she didn't know where they'd get a giant mosquito costume for "Wild Man" and she doubted anyone else would be sporting enough to play the part.

She halfway listened as the old campfire standards about the man with the golden arm and the hook-handed killer were told. Dominic was sitting on Terry's lap with eyes as wide as saucers. She knew she could probably look forward to a sleepless night.

"Ms. Madison?"

Terry's voice shook Beryl out of her reverie. "Yes?"

"You're up."

"Oh...oh...um." She glanced around at the faces of the boys, her eyes finally resting on Duncan. He was staring back expectantly. This obviously had better be a good story if she were not to be an embarrassment to him. Oh, well. She might as well bite the bullet and come up with something scary. It wasn't as if Dominic wouldn't have nightmares already.

She wet her lips and began her story in a whisper. "It was a night much like this one. Cool...crisp...the scent of charcoal and the musty odor of pond muck in the air. If you listened closely enough, you could hear voices calling to you beneath the moaning of the wind. They called to me." She paused for dramatic effect. Each boy leaned in a little closer.

"I was at home alone...reading a murder mystery, in fact...where the butler and the maid had killed their wealthy boss, hacked her to bits and hidden her in the vault behind the picture of a group of dogs playing poker...when suddenly..." She closed her eyes. Actually, she was thinking--but the boys didn't need to know that. "Suddenly, the door blew open. That's when I heard it."

"Heard what, Aunt B?" Duncan asked.

"The voice calling to me beneath the moaning of the wind."

"Who was it?"

"That's what I wanted to know...was compelled to find out. I stood and slowly walked out the door as if in a trance...." She stood and raised her arms out in front of her. "I wondered where I was going...where that voice would lead me...what I would find."

Beryl walked as if she was actually being led by mystical voices. "The moonlight seemed to direct me onto a path leading into the forest. I started that way, but the voice seemed to tell me, 'No, no, no! You're not going in the right direction!'" She spun around and, still holding her arms out like a sleepwalker, she began going in the other direction.

Suddenly she screamed, causing each boy and at least one of the chaperones (Mr. Johnson) to start.

"But no!" she cried. "No! Surely the voice wouldn't lead me here...into the jaws of a monstrous, hungry bear!"

"A bear?" someone echoed.

"What kinda bear?"

"A Kodiak," Beryl said slowly. "The biggest bear there is.... And this bear was the biggest of the biggest." She looked at each rapt face, including Terry's. She had a feeling he knew she was pulling this story out of the air and wanted to see where she'd go with it.

"That bear was looking right at me," Beryl continued. "I was frozen to the ground with fear. I wanted to run, but I couldn't. It was as if I was being held in place by vines which had crept up from beneath the ground and coiled around my ankles. The bear reached an enormous paw toward me, and I closed my eyes, certain that the beast was going to rip my head off. I felt a whoosh of air as that paw clawed the air just centimeters from my face."

Beryl formed a claw with her hand and swished it in front of the boys. She missed Terry's nose by a fraction of an inch.

"It missed," she said as if still surprised. "I wasn't going to give it the opportunity to miss me again. I came to my senses, fought against the invisible vines restraining my feet and ran. But before I'd ran very far, I heard a shot ring out. Was somebody chasing me? Trying to shoot me? I ran deeper into the forest. Another shot rang out...and this time it was more distant."

Beryl lowered her head. "The bear, I thought. Somebody is shooting at the bear. And I turned and went back."

"Why, Aunt B?" Duncan asked.

"Were you afraid?" the boy seated beside Duncan asked.

"Terrified." She sat back down. "More afraid than I'd ever been in my life...but for some reason, I felt a connection and a responsibility to that bear."

"'Cause you're The Flame?" one boy asked.

"Maybe. All I knew was that the bear was no match for a gun. Now the bear was as defenseless before the hunter as I had been before the bear." She shook her head. "I found the bear not far from where I'd left it. It lay dying."

"Where was the hunter?" Terry asked.

"He was gone. I was alone in a small clearing with the bear. It was even angrier than it was before. It tried to claw at me again, but I was able to avoid its blow. I knew it was too weak to get up and chase me, so I stayed. Nothing should die alone. I reached out to stroke its magnificent head, and it snapped its powerful jaws at me...so I didn't bother it anymore. I merely sat beside it thinking that it was a shame that such a majestic animal had to die."

"Suddenly," she raised her voice causing many to jump again, "into the clearing waddled two cubs. They bawled and howled for their mother...and she did for them. Finally, just before she died, she nodded at me...and I knew I would be responsible for those bear cubs for the rest of my life."

It dawned on Beryl that her story had strayed from the eerie. "So, on a clear night...like tonight...when I look up at the sky, I see those two bears...and I know that if I fail them in any way..." She bit her lip. "The mother bear will come back and claw me into a thousand pieces!"

"Gosh," one boy said.

"You never told us that story, Aunt B," Duncan said.

"That's because it's only a ghost story," Beryl said. "It isn't a true story. Did it scare you?"

"Nah," he said, "but I don't scare very easily. It wasn't a bad story though, Aunt B. Good try."

"Thanks." She stood and brushed off the back of her shorts. "Dominic, I think we might ought to go back to the cabin now, don't you?"

"No!" Dominic protested. "I wanna stay wif Terry!"

"It's okay," Terry said. "I'll bring him to the cabin if he gets tired."

"All right then. Goodnight all."

Beryl walked back to the cabin. The moon was full now. It was a beautiful night. Somewhere nearby an owl hooted his hellos to the campers, and the crickets and frogs vied to see who could chirp the loudest. Beryl was grateful for her first moment of peaceful solitude in quite a while.

The first thing Beryl did when she got back to the cabin was run a hot bath in that gloriously deep claw foot tub. She was glad she'd thought to bring along some bubble bath. She dumped three capfuls into the running water. While the tub was filling, she pinned her braid on top of her head, and rummaged through her duffel bag for a novel she'd had for three weeks but had not had time to begin reading. She read the first chapter while the tub was still filling.

At last the tub was filled, and Beryl sank into the warm, jasmine-scented bubbles. She rolled her towel into a neck rest and dove into Chapter Two.

She was wearing out one of the rocking chairs and was well into Chapter Four when Terry tapped on the door. He was carrying a heavy-lidded Dominic over one shoulder. Beryl reached to take Dominic, causing her cropped fleece pajama top to creep up even closer to her ribs, a fact that did not go unnoticed by Terry judging by the direction of his gaze and the slight lift of his brows.

Dominic snuggled into Beryl's arms. "There's not really nowhere wolfs, are they, Aunt B?"

"Of course not, dumpling. There are no such things as werewolves or any of the other scary things you heard about tonight."

"Uh-huh. There's bears. I've seen 'em at the zoo."

"Well, yes, there are bears, but they won't bother you. You're safely tucked in here with me. I won't let anything get you."

"Promise?"

"I promise." She took him over and sat him on his bed. "Let me go thank Terry for taking such good care of you, and I'll be right back, okay?"

"Okay." He lay back against his pillow, and Beryl kissed his downy cheek.

Beryl returned to stand in front of Terry who had closed the door and was leaning nonchalantly against the frame.

"Looks like you put aside your reservations and made yourself at home," Terry observed.

Beryl nodded. "I did."

"It smells great in here." He took a step closer to her. "Is that you?"

"Could be," she said with a shrug.

He moved even closer and bent to nuzzle her neck with his nose. "Yep. It's you, all right."

"Uh..." She jerked her head back in Dominic's direction and silently cursed her sudden shortness of breath. "Don't forget we're not alone."

"He's sound asleep."

"He could be playing possum. Kids do that, you know. Anyway, thanks for keeping an eye on him and bringing him back safely." She crossed in front of Terry and opened the door. "I really appreciate your help. Have a good night, and we'll see you in the morning."

"The bear story...it was about your sister, wasn't it?"

"Oh, of course not. It was a silly story I made up as I went along. Now let's say goodnight before you let the mosquitoes in."

"Goodnight then." He brushed past her. "Too bad we don't have a few more people and a bottle."

6

The first thing on the agenda Saturday morning after breakfast was a nature walk. Beryl doubted that she and Dominic would be able to make the entire excursion, but she figured she knew enough about nature to take him on a different route if need be. For the meantime, however, they were both plodding up a mountain behind Terry who was plodding up the mountain behind the thundering herd of boys. Poor, dilapidated Mr. Johnson, with his one strand of hair greased inadequately over the bald spot that covered most of his head, had elected to stay at camp to ensure against vandalism and thievery.

Just as Beryl was wondering how the boys were going to experience any nature at all with the racket they were making, Ward-Cleaveresque James Appleton ("Jimbo" to the chosen few) blew a whistle and the herd turned as one to see what he was doing.

"Men," James said in a voice right off a car commercial, "I'd like to direct your attention to the flock of ducks gathered in the stream up ahead."

"Wow," a boy named Benny deadpanned.

Undeterred, James reached into his pocket and brought out a sandwich bag containing saltine crackers. "I'll use these to attract the birds to us to allow us a closer inspection."

"Super wow," Benny said.

The other boys looked at Benny as if he'd just shown them Derek Jeter's rookie baseball card. Why are kids so impressed with insolence? Then again, why are kids so impressed with snot?

Beryl chalked each up to another impossible question of the universe and watched as James Appleton's scattered crackers brought on a charge the French Revolutionists would've been proud of. Within seconds, James and the boys were surrounded by ducks snatching crackers off the ground and out of James' hands. The quick ones were greedy. The slow ones were spiteful--they bit the quick ones.

Beryl could see that the ducks scared Dominic, and she quickly swept him up onto her shoulders "where he could see better."

"Ducks are of the family *Anatidae*," James educated, having to shout to be heard over the quacks. "They are of the genus--"

As a hungry slowpoke lunged, James backed away, but not in time. The slowpoke gave Jimbo's hand a nasty, neck-wrenching pinch.

Beryl watched the expressions register across James' face, and had to admire the way he obviously thought--but did not say--some very un-Ward-Cleaveresque words. The boys naturally found the entire ordeal hilarious because it was Mr. Appleton's hand that was bitten and not one of theirs.

"Let's move on," James croaked at last, and led the boys toward some interesting-looking flora (Beryl prayed it was not poison oak). The ungrateful ducks waddled behind their benefactors in hopes of another handout.

"So, is Mr. Appleton the science teacher?" Beryl asked Terry.

He grinned. "No. He's an accountant. And he's Benny's dad."

"As in 'wow, super wow' Benny?"

"You got it. I admire James - he's really trying to win the boy over."

"Why is he having to?"

"The parents divorced--apparently a messy ordeal--and Benny blames his dad."

"Where the ducks go?" Dominic asked.

"They followed Mr. Appleton and his crackers, sweetheart."

"Can we go, too?"

"Sure," Beryl said. "Mr. Goodson, will you lead the way?"

"I'll lead," he said softly. "The question is, will you follow?"

"I suppose that depends on where we're going."

He smiled, and there was an unspoken message in his eyes

that Beryl chose to ignore.

"Let's not follow the crowd," he suggested. "Let's see what we can find on our own."

"Okay." Beryl put Dominic down. He walked between Beryl and Terry. Beryl slipped her hand into Dominic's and was surprised when Dominic gave his other hand to Terry. A casual observer would believe them to be a happy little family.

They walked over a hill and found a cluster of wildflowers. Butterflies fluttered over the heads of pink, white, and yellow blossoms. With a gasp, Dominic jerked his hands away from Beryl and Terry and scampered down the hill and dove into the flowers.

Terry took his cell phone from his pocket and quickly snapped a photo.

"Text that to me, would you please?" Beryl asked , pleasantly surprised by his wanting to capture the moment. She'd felt that way herself, but then, Dominic was her nephew...practically, her child. Terry had simply beaten her to the draw.

Dominic sat up and favored them with a wide, open-mouthed smile when a butterfly landed on his knee. Terry snapped another picture.

"He's precious," Beryl said, as much to herself as to Terry.

"He certainly is. He must come from good stock." Terry walked down the hill, bent and picked a daisy. Returning to Beryl's side, he ran the flower gently down the side of her face. "For you."

"Ah," she said with a grin, "but does he love me or love me not?"

"Don't ruin the flower to see. I can assure you he loves you."

"Look at me, Aunt B!" Dominic yelled.

Beryl looked past Terry to see what antics Dominic was performing for her now. He'd plucked a pink, fringed petal flower and put it behind his ear.

"Look," he repeated, "like that girl in that movie!"

Beryl and Terry laughed.

"Yes, he does love me," Beryl said. With a wink at Terry, she tucked the daisy behind her ear.

As soon as the group returned from the nature walk, Mr. Johnson greeted them at the picnic shelter with a box of crafting materials.

"Boys," he announced effusively, "together we are going to

make each of you a craft you'll be delighted to take home to your mothers tomorrow! Gather round, please."

Beryl held her arms out to Dominic, who had switched over to ride on Terry's shoulders during the latter part of the nature walk. "Come on, dumpling," she said. "Let's go back to the cabin to rest before lunch."

"No! I wanna make sumpin for my mama! For when she gets home!"

"I'll help Dominic," Terry told Beryl. "Why don't you go on back to the cabin and relax for a little while?"

"I'll walk with you, Ms. Madison," James Appleton said, with an over-the-shoulder glance at his bad-tempered son. "I don't think I'm particularly welcome here right now."

"I understand," she said, as they began walking toward the cabins.

"Do you?" James asked.

"I think so. Terry told me that Benny is your son, and that you and his mother are divorced."

"That's right. It was nobody's fault really--we merely grew up and grew away from each other, I guess--but Benny still blames me."

"He has to blame somebody."

"But why? Why does he have to blame anybody?"

"So he can be sure he's not to blame himself, I suppose. I'll bet if you dig a little deeper, you'll find that he fears the divorce really was his fault."

James smiled sadly. "Maybe you're right."

"I doubt it," Beryl said, returning his smile. "But there's my two cents, and that's about what my advice is worth."

They'd reached the cabins now, and were preparing to go their separate ways.

"Thanks for listening, Ms. Madison."

"Beryl. And thank you for helping me keep my cool and refrain from throttling Mr. Johnson for being so thoughtless."

"Thoughtless?" James echoed.

"Yes, thoughtless. Doesn't he realize that Duncan and Dominic...and maybe some of the other children...don't have mothers?"

He closed his eyes and brought a hand up to his temple. "Oh, no. I'm sorry. I'm sure Mr. Johnson meant well."

"I know he did," Beryl said with a sigh. "And I know the boys are going to face not having a mother or a father from now on...every Mother's Day, every Father's Day...every day, but I just wasn't prepared for it today...and I didn't prepare them for it either."

"How could you have prepared them, Beryl?"

"I don't know."

A scream shattered the regret-filled silence and reverberated through the trees.

"Dominic," Beryl breathed, as she raced back to the picnic shelter.

"It's all right," Terry said as Beryl sprinted into the clearing.

"Let me see! Let me see him!" She didn't stop running until she was at Dominic's side.

Terry had the child on his lap trying to soothe him, and when he pulled away to allow Beryl to examine Dominic, she saw that there was blood on Terry's shirt.

"Oh, dear lord!" she cried. "I'm so sorry."

"Beryl, calm down," Terry said firmly. "It's not as bad as it looks."

"Not as--"

Terry's warning scowl quelled the remainder of her sentence. He was right. She knew that. To react this way now would only frighten Dominic more...and Duncan, too, for that matter.

She looked away from Dominic long enough to see that Duncan was there at his brother's other side, tears brimming in his eyes, face stark and looking much older than its seven years.

"Oh, you're right," she said, soothing Dominic's hair with a trembling hand. "You're right, T—er, Mr. Goodson. It isn't so bad at all. It's only a little cut...but since it's so near your eye, dumpling, I think we should go into town and let a doctor have a look at it."

"No!" Dominic wailed.

Beryl took him from Terry and cradled him against her shoulder. "It's all right, sweetheart. You'll be fine. I'll be with you every second, and I won't let anyone hurt you."

"Promise?"

"I promise, angel. I promise."

"I'll drive you," Terry said.

"I'm goin', too," Duncan asserted.

Mr. Johnson produced a mangled bandage from the bottom

of his craft box, but Beryl distastefully rejected it, telling him she'd prefer to use the neckerchief Duncan had already provided.

Mr. Appleton took charge of the boys, efficiently quieting them and directing them back to their crafts, while Terry shepherded Beryl, Dominic and Duncan into Beryl's car.

Beryl gently rocked Dominic until he'd stopped crying. "It's all right, sweetheart. It's all right. What a brave boy you are."

"Yeah," Duncan chimed in from the back seat. "You're brave. All the guys think so, too."

"They do?" Dominic asked.

"They sure do. I'm lucky to have a brother like you, right, Aunt B?"

"You sure are," Beryl agreed. "And I'm lucky to have you both."

"And I'm just happy to be here," Terry said, breaking the seriousness of the moment and making them all laugh.

"I'm glad you're here, too," Beryl said, closing her eyes and rocking Dominic again.

At the emergency room, Terry took control of signing Dominic in and relating what had happened. He asked Beryl for her insurance card, and she produced it from her wallet before she resumed rocking Dominic. At this point, she didn't know if she was really rocking to comfort Dominic or herself.

"They need to know who--besides you--they can contact in case of an emergency," Terry asked Beryl.

Her eyes widened. "An emergency? You think--"

"It's only a precaution, Beryl. Only a precaution."

"Right," she said, her shoulders slumping with relief. "A precaution, that's all. Um, Mama...Molly Madison--have them put her down. I need to call her."

"All right."

"My cell phone is in the car."

"After they've finished filling out the paperwork, I'll run out and get it for you."

"Thank you."

Molly answered the phone on the first ring.

"Mama?" Beryl was unable to keep the tremor out of her voice.

"What's wrong, baby?"

"We're at the emergency room...uh...near Camp Wannameyer. Dominic fell and cut his eye."

"Is it bad?"

"I don't know, Mama."

"I'm on my way."

"No...that's okay. Everything is under control."

"I'm on my way," Molly reasserted.

"But what about Daddy?"

"I'll call his friend Bill to come and sit with him."

"But what if--"

"Goodbye, Beryl. I'll see you in a few minutes."

As Beryl dropped the phone into her purse, a nurse called Dominic's name. After what seemed an interminable wait in the tiny exam room, a young doctor with a goatee and a ring through one nostril breezed into the room.

"Hey, champ," the doctor said. "What's up?"

Dominic said nothing, but rather, cowered against Beryl.

"He fell and cut his eye," Beryl said.

"How?" the doctor asked.

"He tripped and fell against a picnic table," Terry supplied.

"I see."

Beryl angled her head to get a look at the doctor's nameplate. His name was, appropriately enough, Dr. Young.

"Come on, champ," Dr. Young said, gently pulling Dominic away from Beryl. "Let's see what we've got."

"No!" Dominic wailed.

"All right, all right. You can stay with Mama; I just need her to put you on the other hip so I can see that boo-boo."

No one corrected the doctor's assumption.

Beryl positioned Dominic on her left hip in order to give the doctor access to the wound.

Dr. Young looked cross-eyed at Dominic and lolled out his tongue. Dominic giggled. The doctor took a cotton ball saturated with hydrogen peroxide and cleansed the wound.

"This isn't bad at all," Dr. Young said. "I'd say two stitches will do it."

"Stitches?" Beryl asked. "Isn't there some other way?"

"I've heard about a glue you can use," Terry said.

"Well, yeah, I can use the glue...it's just that--because of his age--you'll have to watch that he doesn't pick at it or it could get infected."

"Let's go with the glue," Beryl said. "He won't pick at it. He's a big boy."

"All right," Dr. Young said. He opened a drawer and removed a tube of something that looked suspiciously like super glue. "I need you to hold perfectly still, champ."

Beryl braced Dominic's head against her own and held her breath as the doctor dabbed the glue onto the cut.

"Okay," Dr. Young said. "You're good to go. Now, Mom, don't soak the area or use any antibiotic ointments or anything like that on it; and Dad, make sure he keeps those little hands away from it. Any questions?"

Beryl and Terry both dumbly shook their heads. Then, with a nod, Dr. Young breezed out.

Beryl's eyes cut to Terry, then to the floor, the walls, the ceiling, anywhere but at Terry until the nurse brought Dominic's discharge slip. For the doctor to think Beryl was the boys' mother was to draw a natural conclusion. But to think Terry was their father? That was outrageous. Right?

Molly jumped up out of her chair the moment they entered the lobby. "How are Grandma's guys?" she asked casually, though Beryl could see that her sharp eyes were examining Dominic's face.

"We're better now," Duncan said. "Aren't we, Dominic?"

"Yeah. Better now."

"Molly Madison, this is Terry Goodson, Duncan's teacher."

"Ah, yes," Molly said, extending her right hand, "the one who thinks we're all nuts."

"Mama!" Beryl chided.

Terry laughed, taking Molly's hand and planting a kiss on it rather than giving her the handshake she'd anticipated. "It's a pleasure to meet you, Mrs. Madison."

"Better watch this one," Molly quipped. "He's a charmer." She reached and took Dominic from Beryl. "And so's this one. How'd you like to go home with me tonight?"

"I wanna go back at camp."

"Suit yourself, then," Molly said. "Do they have fudge brownie sundaes at camp?"

Dominic shook his dark head.

"Popcorn?"

Another slow head shake.

"The cowboy movie?"

"Aunt B-B head, can I go wif Gwandma?"

"I don't know," Beryl said. "Mama, how can you--"

"I can, that's how. It'll be great to have Dominic there tonight. And tomorrow morning, we can have strawberry muffins and cereal with banana...."

"And maybe a waffle?" Dominic asked.

"Maybe," Molly said. Her gaze encompassed Duncan and Beryl. "We'll see you tomorrow afternoon."

"Okay," Beryl said, "We'll see you tomorrow afternoon, Duncan. I'll pick you up at--"

"You can't leave," Molly and Duncan said in unison.

"Aunt B, if you go, we won't have enough chaperones, and we'll all have to go home."

"Oh, Duncan, I don't think one chaperone more or less matters at this point," Beryl said. "Do you, Terry?"

"Actually, it would, but you need to do what's best for Dominic." Terry looked at Duncan. "And the rest of us will have to be men about it if the trip is cut short."

"Aw, man!" Duncan kicked at a floor tile with the toe of his tennis shoe.

"Go on back to camp with Duncan," Molly said. "I'm selfish. Ralph and I want Dominic to ourselves for a little while."

"But, Mama, if you need me--"

"I'll call," Molly finished. "We'll see you guys tomorrow. Nice meeting you, Mr. Goodson."

"Ditto, Mrs. Madison."

It was nearly dinnertime when they returned to the campsite. Duncan returned to his cabin to regale his friends with his account of how they glued his little brother back together. Terry went to check about dinner preparations. Beryl went to her cabin. There she sank to the floor just inside the doorway and wept.

That's how Terry found her a few minutes later.

"Hey, hey, it's all right." He pushed the door closed with his foot and sat down beside her.

She offered no resistance when he pulled her onto his lap. He brushed her hair away from her face. "It's all over now."

"No...it's...not." Her words came out in gulping sobs.

"Of course, it is."

"You...don't...understand."

"Then explain it to me."

Beryl took a deep, tremulous breath. "This is all my fault. Ron and August couldn't have left the boys with anyone less competent." She swatted at her tears with her index fingers. "I'm a stupid failure! I couldn't even watch Dominic long enough to keep him from getting hurt."

She shoved herself up off Terry's lap and strode across the room. "As an aunt, I was 'way cool'. As a substitute mother, I'm a big zero!"

In two long strides, Terry had bridged the space between them and spun Beryl around to face him. "A big zero? You think you're a big zero? The boys wouldn't have been able to come on this camping trip if not for you. You came to my office last Monday in a ridiculous—albeit sexy—costume because Duncan meant too much to you to miss the appointment." He gave her shoulders a slight shake. "Where do you get off thinking you're a failure?"

"Because I am! Because I can't do this, Terry! I can't cook, I can't protect them from getting hurt, I can't be their mother!"

"You're all they've got. They miss their mother because she was their mother, and they miss their father for the same reason." He pulled her to him and wrapped his arms around her solidly. "They love their parents, Beryl; but they love you, too. And if anybody could have protected Dominic from falling, I would have. I reached for him, but I didn't make it in time."

"I should've been there," Beryl whispered raggedly.

"You can't follow them around forever. They have to take their licks just like you did when you were growing up."

"I know, but...I don't want them to ever be hurt again."

"And you think you aren't a good mother."

Beryl pulled away enough to search Terry's eyes for any scorn or sarcasm. Not a trace. She saw only kindness, sympathy...and maybe a little something else.

He dug his hands into her hair and pressed his body against hers.

Okay, a lot of something else.

It was Beryl's last coherent thought before Terry's mouth covered hers.

7

Beryl had never wanted a man so badly in her life. She knew better than to get involved with one of Duncan's teachers. If things fell through, she'd still have to deal with the man the rest of the year. More importantly, if things fell through, it would be one more heartache for Duncan and Dominic. She wouldn't do that to them.

She needed to tell Terry to stop.... And yet the things he was doing to her body felt so wonderful, she didn't want him to ever stop. His mouth seared a path from her earlobe down her throat.

"Terry, we can't do this."

"Oh, but we can." He kissed her deeply. "Beryl, please tell me you want this, too."

"I do want this," she said, "but--."

He placed his mouth over hers, silencing her with his kiss. He picked her up, and she could feel the evidence of his desire as he lay with her on the bed. He kissed her and ran his hands over her in a frenzied hunger, and she responded with more passion than she'd ever felt in her life. He unfastened her shorts, and the sound of the snap popping open bolted into Beryl's consciousness like a thunderclap.

"We cannot do this!" Beryl sat up and refastened her shorts. "I can't have the boys' aunt being known as the biggest slut around." She buried her face in her hands as fresh sobs racked her body. "How could I be so selfish and so stupid?"

"You're human, Beryl," Terry said. "Desire is not something to

67

be ashamed of."

"For two people in our position it is." She raised her head. "Or it should be. I have a responsibility to Duncan and Dominic, as well as to the kids at this camp, to be thinking of their welfare, not taking a tumble with one of the other chaperones."

"Beryl, it's not--"

"What? It's not like that? It is as exactly like that!"

"Will you please listen to me? I--"

"No. Not right now." She waved him away with a trembling hand. "I need to be alone, and you need to see to your scouts."

Terry ran both hands through his hair and blew out a long breath. "I didn't mean for—"

"Please go." Beryl hid her face in her hands again. When she had the courage to lift her head again, Terry was gone.

She curled up on the bed and cried herself to sleep.

When she woke up, it was dark. She stretched her arms up over her head. She could hear the boys off in the distance, so she knew it wasn't lights out yet. But it was close…. Some chaperone she turned out to be. Still, she was too ashamed to make an appearance tonight. In the morning she'd put on her The Flame persona and stride to breakfast like she owned the place. And she'd chaperone her little heart out. Tonight she wanted nothing more than to hide.

She threw back the covers, got off the bed, and went into the bathroom. She turned the faucets on the bathtub so that the water would be a bit on the hot side—as in, "hot as Hell." The Hell she would most assuredly burn in if one of those kids had interrupted her and Terry in the throes of passion this afternoon. This was a lovely situation. Absolutely lovely.

Beryl added two extra capfuls of bubble bath to the water. She took the candle from the living room and put it on the wooden towel rack above the tub. Now all she needed was music. She'd studied Stress Relief 101—this was nothing new to her.

She slunk back into the bedroom and dug her radio out of one of the duffel bags. She'd have preferred a little Adele, but as it was only an am/fm radio, she guessed she'd have to take what she could get. She was in luck. She found a classical station that was playing some very slow, very soothing music.

She gathered her bubbles about her like a foamy blanket and put one leg up on the side of the tub. She leaned her head back against the tub and closed her eyes. She hummed along with Bach's

"Sheep May Safely Graze."

"Oh, my."

Beryl's eyes sprang open. Her mouth followed suit, and she emitted a scream that would've made Wild Man proud.

"J-James Appleton!" Beryl squeaked, slipping further down into the tub and grabbing a towel. He'd turned his back, but she didn't know how long she could count on his sense of honor and duty to stay that way. "What're you doing here?"

"Beryl, it's me," Terry said from the living room. "I heard you scream. What's the matter?"

Beryl groaned. "Don't come in here."

Too late.

"What's going on?" Terry demanded--hands on hips--as soon as he stepped into the doorway of the bathroom and met Jimbo face to face.

"I...I noticed Ms. Madison didn't...wasn't at dinner." He took a small sandwich bag out of his pocket and held it in the air for Beryl to see. "I brought you some granola."

"Thanks," Beryl said through clenched teeth. "Could you just leave it on the sink please?" She looked at Terry. "And everything is fine, so you can be on your way too."

"So...so sorry to interrupt," James said, moving slowly out of the room. "I'll walk back with you, Goodson."

"Yeah." Terry said.

This is perfect. Two men at camp have just seen me naked.

Beryl got out of the tub, wrapped herself in a sky blue terry robe, got back into her bed and tried to regain some peace of mind by escaping into her novel.

It was not to be.

"What now?" she yelled when there was a knock on the door. She threw back the covers and stomped to the living room. "Who is it, and what do you want?"

"It's me," Terry answered glumly. "Can I come in?"

"No!"

"I want to apologize."

"Apology accepted. Now go away."

"Look, I just--"

Beryl heard him pound his fist against the door. Then he was gone.

The next morning Beryl dressed with extra care, although all she had to wear was the white tee shirt and jean shorts she'd brought for this day. She would have liked to wear a long dress and veil or at least a turtleneck and jeans, but just as the saying goes, "you have to dance with the one that brought you," you also have to "dance in the dress you brought." Okay, it was utter nonsense, but her mind was shot and she just wanted to get through the morning and go home.

Still, she took more pains than usual with her hair and makeup. Anything to stall. This morning, she'd taken her hair out of the French braid Raife had put it in, washed it and then spritzed it with a leave-in conditioner and pushed it off her forehead with a tortoiseshell headband. The bulk of her thick hair hung in spirals about her shoulders.

She looked in the mirror, trying to summon the courage to go up to the dining area to help with breakfast. She squeezed her eyes shut and took a deep breath. She could do this. She could. All she had to do was pretend it was some improv for the show.

Yeah, that's it. Wild Man was somewhere in that forest like some sort of Fagin trying to get these scouts to steal for him. Only The Flame could protect the children and foil Wild Man's evil scheme. Beryl shouldered The Flame's persona like a suit of armor and headed for the battlefield.

She walked slowly to the picnic area. She smelled sausage grilling. The sun was brightening the sky with red orange streaks. Meadowlarks and robins were singing their morning songs. The butterflies in Beryl's stomach were doing somersaults. She scanned the perimeters of the forest to remind herself of the mindset she'd psyched herself into before leaving her cabin.

I can do this. I can do this.

Just her luck: Terry, James Appleton, and Mr. Johnson were all gathered around the grill. They turned as a group as she approached. Beryl wondered if there was something to that pheromone thing after all.

"Good morning, gentlemen," she said brightly. "I'm sorry I'm late."

"Not at all! Not at all," James said, nearly tripping in his haste to get to her. "The truth of the matter is, the rest of us got here early. I suppose we're all eager to get home...in one way." He cocked his dark head and gave her a sidelong, puppy-eyed look. "I'm sure we will all miss you, though, Ms. Madison, and your magnoliaceous grace."

Beryl frowned. "Thank you...I think."

"*Magnoliaceous*?" Mr. Johnson harped, peering over top of his black framed glasses at James. "What in the world does that mean? You forget, Appleton, that not all of us obtained a double major with one of those being science. If you intend to tell the woman she's like a magnolia or something, why can't you just say so?"

"I did say so, Johnson," James said evenly.

"Mr. Goodson," Beryl said, "do you need any help over there?"

"No, thank you, Ms. Madison," Terry said. "I've got it under control."

The troops began straggling to the picnic area.

"Somethin' smells halfway decent," Benny said. He stumbled over to the plates and picked one up.

Benny obviously was not a morning person. His camouflage shirt and shorts looked as if they'd been slept in, and an orange hat was pulled down over his ears. The hair that sprouted in all directions from under the hat looked as if it wouldn't recognize a comb if one came up and launched an attack on his head.

Hard to believe this was James Appleton's son. Beryl looked over at James who was pouring orange juice into plastic cups. He winked.

Neat, attractive, genial "Jimbo" looked as if he could've been doing a juice commercial in his navy polo shirt and khaki shorts. Beryl could even imagine the jingle: *Greet your guests...'vite 'em in...'c' 'em to the table. Give 'em juice...orange you glad...there's "fresh-squeezed" on the label?*

Duncan broke her reverie. "Hi, Aunt B. How's Dominic?"

"He's doing great. I called Grandma earlier this morning and she said that Dominic was still asleep. The two of them stayed up late last night watching movies and eating popcorn."

"What movies did they watch?"

"I don't know."

"Probably *Angels in the Outfield* and *Shane*. *Shane* is one of Grandpa's favorites."

"And yours, too," Beryl reminded.

"Yeah...." He began eating eggs and sausage that appeared to have the consistency of rubber. "Maybe I can spend the night with

Grandma and Grandpa sometime soon."

"I'm sure they'd love that."

"Ain'tcha hungry, Aunt B?"

"No, Duncan. I'm fine, thanks."

"But you didn't eat supper last night, and now you ain't--"

"Aren't."

"--eating breakfast. You sick or something?"

"No. I was upset about Dominic getting hurt, that's all. You can bet I'll eat a good lunch when we get to Grandma's. By the way, do you wanna ride home with me in the Camaro?"

"Well, no, Aunt B. I'm ridin' back with the guys. I'm jeopardizing my status being seen talking to you as it is."

"Oh, well, gee. Let me see if I can find something else to do."

Beryl got up just as Terry sat down at their table with a heaping plate of scrambled eggs and sausage. His food looked even more rubbery than Duncan's.

"Don't leave on my account," Terry said.

"It's not because of you, Mr. Goodson. She's mad at me." Duncan rolled his eyes. "Women."

"I'm not mad at you," Beryl said. "I just have some tidying up left to do at the cabin, and I wouldn't want to jeopardize your status for anything in the world."

"See what I mean?" Duncan asked Terry.

"Exactly."

Beryl was in her cabin stuffing her toiletries into a duffel bag when Terry dropped in. He looked terrific today--as always--in a red tee shirt and black shorts.

"Thought I'd come see if you need any help," he said.

"I'm doing fine." She resumed packing. "But thanks for offering."

He put his hands in his pockets and leaned against the doorframe. "I wanted to apologize about last night...yesterday...everything. You were right. I certainly didn't act very professional."

Beryl paused, holding her blow dryer in mid-stuff. "Neither did I. I...I don't usually behave that way."

Terry nodded. "I know."

Beryl wedged the dryer into the bag, wondering what he meant by that--that he was such a good lover he could charm the pants off anybody or that yesterday's behavior was exceptional for both of them? She chose not to ask.

Terry removed his hands from his pockets so he could spread them in an encompassing gesture. "I was coming back to apologize last night--the first time--when I heard you scream. That's how I caught you in the tub. I'm sorry for that, too."

"You don't get it, do you?" Beryl asked on a sigh. "It's not only because of a sense of modesty that I'm embarrassed about our--" She looked over her shoulder toward the open door to ensure they weren't being overheard. "--behavior yesterday or the fact that two men came in on me while I was bathing." She searched Terry's face for some sign of understanding. "I'm responsible for two little boys now. How people look at me affects how people look at them, and I won't have anyone looking down at my children."

"Beryl, we didn't do anything wrong. We're two people who are attracted to each other--two single people." He stepped closer. "We didn't let things get too far out of control--"

"But had anyone caught us, it would have been 'Way to go, Terry!' and 'That Madison girl is a tramp. What a bad influence she must be on those poor boys.'"

"Aw, come on."

"It's true. You know it is."

"Okay, so now what? Where do we go from here?"

She looked at her watch. "Home, in about an hour."

"That's not what I'm talking about, and you know it. Damn it, Beryl, I'm attracted to you and you're attracted to me. Now what're we gonna do about it?"

Beryl cocked her head and studied the ceiling above Terry's head as if looking for an answer in the tiny cobweb in the corner. No grain of wisdom there. Obviously, this wasn't Charlotte's web. "Nothing."

"Nothing?"

She brought her eyes back down to his. "It's not because I don't want to be with you, Terry. I do. Six or seven months ago, we could've gotten together and had a great time for as long as we both wanted to be together. Then we could've gone our separate ways and wished each other well." She shook her head. "I can't do that now."

"Why not?"

"Because when we go our separate ways, Duncan and Dominic lose you, too. They've lost too much in their young lives already."

"Give me a chance. How do you know we'll go our separate ways?"

"For Pete's sake, you hold over your kitchen sink to eat. You told me, Raife, and the children only three nights ago that you wouldn't need any furniture until you were ready to settle down many, many years from now."

"I'll admit I said that, but...things change."

"That's not a chance I can take right now."

"So, what? You're never going on another date unless you know you'll end up married to the guy?" He flipped his palms up. "What're you going to do? Take the guy to a psychic before you go out with him? See if she sees orange blossoms and wedding bells in her crystal ball before you sit down to a meal with him?"

Beryl didn't answer. She turned her back to him and began folding her robe.

Terry stepped in front of her and snatched the robe out of her hands. "What if you get fooled? What if the wedding bells means he has a brother who's getting married or something?"

Beryl still didn't answer. She kept her eyes on the floor.

"What I'm trying to say is that there are no guarantees in this world, Beryl!"

"I know!" She finally looked up at him, tears shimmering in her eyes. "So I can't afford to take any chances, now can I?"

Terry shoved the robe back into her hands. "I guess not."

When she heard the door click signaling Terry's departure, she buried her face in the robe and cried.

She wasn't crying when she left the cabin, however. She'd reapplied her makeup and plastered on a smile. James promptly met her outside her cabin, begged her forgiveness for his rudeness in barging in on her the night before, and carried her bags to the Camaro.

Beryl threw herself into cleaning the dining area as if nothing else mattered in the world except that the dining area be spotless when she left it...or, at least, as spotless as it had been when she'd found it. When she finished, she was still smiling.

On the drive back to the school, Beryl tried to blast Terry out of her mind by cranking up some hard rock music. When they arrived at school, she turned off the radio. She was still smiling.

James and Benny got into a maroon Mercedes. James waved goodbye. She waved back. Still smiling.

Duncan got in the Camaro. Terry got into his silver bachelor-mobile and drove away without even glancing in her direction. Even then, she was still smiling.

She reached for her cell phone, called Molly, and said, "Mama, can the boys and I stay with you tonight?"

"Uh-oh," Molly said. "Ice cream night?"

"You got it."

8

As soon as Ralph and the boys were asleep, Molly propelled Beryl into the kitchen, opened the freezer and took out a half-gallon of Moose Tracks ice cream. She put the carton of ice cream and two spoons on the table.

"Okay," she said, pulling out a chair for Beryl and sitting in the chair to her left. "I know this has something to do with that sexy school teacher."

Beryl sank into the chair and took the top off the ice cream carton. "How do you know that?" She dug a spoon into the ice cream.

"'Cause if I was your age, he's what I'd have on my mind." Molly spooned out a tiny, chocolate-covered peanut butter cup and savored it before asking: "So, did you sleep with him?"

Beryl would've choked had she not known her mother so well. Instead, she slowly took another bite of ice cream. "No."

"But you wanted to?"

"I can't believe I was such an idiot. Mama, I nearly made love to that man in a cabin with Duncan not a hundred yards away."

Molly frowned, poked a strip of fudge into her mouth, and chewed thoughtfully. "Which means you wanted him pretty badly. Is this a lust thing, or is there more to it?"

She laid down her spoon and put her chin on her hands. "I don't know. He's a confirmed bachelor...and he likes it that way."

"How do you know?"

Beryl sighed. "I just know. And I can't risk Duncan and Dominic starting to care for someone and then suffering another loss."

"Mmmm." Molly nodded. "And that goes for you, too, doesn't it?"

Beryl shrugged. "Maybe."

She gave Beryl her mother-knows-best smile.

"Okay, yeah," Beryl admitted. "I don't want to be just another notch in Terry Goodson's bedpost either."

"So what do you want to be to Terry Goodson?"

Beryl grabbed her spoon and dove back into the ice cream. "I don't know."

"The Gemstones are a heck of a lot more fun to draw than Wild Man," Raife said.

He was sitting at Beryl's kitchen table creating pages for a new coloring book for "The Flame."

"I imagine so," Beryl said, not looking up from her task of scanning the finished pictures into her computer. She could feel Raife's eyes boring into her back, but she shrugged him off, and began printing out fifty copies of one of the pictures.

"What's up with you today?" Raife asked.

"Just trying to get as many of these done as possible before Duncan gets home."

"Not picking him up today?"

"No. He's riding the bus. You know he always rides the bus on Monday."

"I know he usually does, but I thought that after this weekend, you might want to pick him up so you could see Mr. Good One."

"The name's Goodson, and no."

"Ah, then, therein lies the rub, eh?"

Beryl turned at last. "So, what've you got on that one?" She nodded at the drawing on which he was still working.

"Opal with her hand in the jewel case."

She got up to give the picture a closer inspection. "Looks good."

"Don't change the subject. What happened with you and Mr. Hottie, this weekend?"

"Raife, there's nothing going on with Terry and me." That much was true. "But speaking of him reminds me of his audit which reminds me of Bob March. Have you heard anything about him lately?"

"How your mind can switch gears from Mr. Hottie to Bob March that quickly is beyond me." He pushed a lock of hair behind his ear. "I don't know of anything current, but there's always some kind of rumors circulating about March. I can check in to it if you want me to."

"No...no, thanks. But, you know, ever since doing that audit, I've been meaning to go back over the accountings for August's and Ron's estates."

"Baby girl, what's the point? Why dredge all that up again? You'll only upset yourself."

"Maybe, but--"

The computer alerted Beryl to its need for a paper refill, and the doorbell rang.

"Raife, could you please get that while I refill the paper tray?"

"Sure."

He returned with a basket of flowers. It was beautiful. Stargazer lilies, heather, and gladiolus were artfully arranged among dark green fern fronds.

"Nothing to tell about this weekend, eh?"

"Nothing at all." Beryl reached for the envelope pinned to the large yellow bow. As she opened it, she tried to appear nonchalant. Rather than being from Terry, the flowers were from James Appleton. *Darn.* The card read, "A thousand apologies. James."

"Not from whom you'd hoped?" Raife asked.

"What?" She put the card back into the envelope. "They're from a friend, that's all."

"Yeah, just not the right 'friend.' I won't aggravate you about it, but if you need to talk about anything at all, you know I'm here for you, right?"

"Of course, I do. Thank you."

It had been nice of James to send her flowers, Beryl supposed. She'd call and thank him later...at a time when she was sure she'd get his answering machine.

As Beryl and Raife were putting together the fiftieth coloring book, Duncan burst through the front door and into the living room. Beryl heard his backpack land on the floor with a thud and hurriedly completed the binding on the last book.

"Aunt B," Duncan said, stomping into the kitchen and dropping into a chair, "you can't go on no more boy trips with us."

"Why not?" Beryl asked. "Did I do something wrong?"

Duncan sighed. "You make the boys act stupid."

Raife stifled a chuckle.

"What do you mean?" Beryl asked, frowning.

"All the boys watched your show before coming to school this morning, and Benny Appleton said his dad even watched it with him. Mr. Goodson heard us talking about it and said he saw your show this morning, too."

"Why is that bad? You wanted the boys to like me, didn't you?"

"Sure, Aunt B, but I wanted them to like you so they'd like me. Instead, they just like you."

"Oh, honey, they don't. They just--" Her eyes pleaded for Raife to help her.

"They're just using your Aunt B as something in common for you guys to talk about. In a day or two, it'll be something else."

"Ya think?" Duncan asked.

"I sure do. Why else would they--and their dads--be watching a show about some dumb girl running around in a stupid costume?"

"Yeah." Duncan smiled. "You're right."

"Go get washed up," Beryl said. "As a way of making up with you, I'll take you and Dominic out to eat tonight."

"All right!"

Beryl waited until she heard Duncan's feet pounding up the stairs. "Dumb girl in a stupid costume?"

"It worked, didn't it?" Raife laughed as he linked his hands behind his head and raised his dark brows mockingly. "And it's painfully obvious that absolutely *nothing* went on during that camping trip this weekend. But why don't we make fifty more coloring books on Friday anyway. For some reason, you're really in demand." He picked up one of the books and leafed through it. "I've got a feeling these things will sell like purple boas at a Gay Pride parade."

"Weren't you just leaving?"

"Actually, yes, I was." He stood and kissed the top of Beryl's head. "Maybe you'll tell me one of these days what didn't happen on that camping trip."

Ignoring his jibe, Beryl walked him to the door. As Raife was leaving, Terry pulled into the driveway in his gleaming silver BMW, a/k/a the bachelor-mobile. Beryl folded her arms and waited at the door to see what he wanted.

"Hi," he called as he approached the porch.

"Hi," Beryl said.

"Duncan left his workbook at school this afternoon. I was afraid he'd miss it and think he'd lost it."

Beryl took the book Terry extended. "Thank you. How much homework does he have tonight?"

"Oh...none." He put his hands in the pockets of his gray slacks. "It's just that Duncan likes to take all his books home every day." He shrugged. "I don't know why--but he does. Some kids do that. He's...he's one of them."

"Thanks for bringing this by. I'll give it to him." Trying not to notice how devastatingly handsome he looked in his navy sport jacket and light blue polo shirt, Beryl turned to go inside.

"Beryl, wait."

She turned, her brows raised in question.

"Can I come in...just for a second?"

"I'm afraid not. Duncan and I were just leaving to pick up Dominic, and then we're going out to dinner."

"Look, I want to apologize again for--"

"For what? You were a comfort to me when I was upset, that's all. No biggie."

"But--"

"Let's go!" Duncan said, bounding into the living room. "Grab my purse, please. It's beside the couch."

"Hey, Mr. Goodson. What're you doing here?"

"I--"

"He brought your workbook. He was afraid you'd think you lost it. Wasn't that nice?"

"Yeah...but I left it in my desk today on purpose. My backpack is gettin' too heavy."

"Oh," Terry said. "I'm sorry. I...I didn't realize that."

"Well, that's okay. See ya tomorrow."

"Your Aunt B tells me you guys are going out to dinner."

"Yes," Beryl said, looking pointedly at her watch. "And we'd better hurry before Little Rascals sets Dominic out on the stoop by himself."

"You guys have a good time," Terry said. "I guess I'd better go grab some dinner myself." He turned and walked slowly off the porch.

"Do you want to go with us?" Duncan asked.

Terry turned, trapping Beryl with his gaze. "No. I wouldn't want to intrude."

"You wouldn't be," Beryl said, perpetually confounded by this man who, one minute she wanted to grab by the hand and run away with, and the next minute, shove away. "We'd love for you to go with us."

He smiled. "Then I'd love to go."

Dominic was thrilled to see Terry. In fact, as soon as they arrived at Little Rascal's, he threw his little body into Terry's arms instead of Beryl's.

"Whachu doin' here?" Dominic asked.

"I'm going to dinner with you, Duncan, and your aunt. Is that all right with you?"

"Yeah!" He planted a big, smacking kiss on Terry's cheek, and Terry stood up with Dominic still wound around his neck.

"Then let's go."

The boys chose a Mexican restaurant where the dark, mustachioed maître d' kept referring to Beryl as *bonita senora*. The boys ate tacos until Beryl thought they would be sick, while she and Terry munched on chimichangas and nachos with salsa.

They returned to Beryl's house after dinner, and Dominic insisted that Terry stay and watch a *Gilligan's Island* rerun with them.

"I like Gilligan," Dominic said during a commercial break. "He's silly."

"I've always been partial to Ginger," Terry said, with a pointed glance at Beryl over top of the child's head.

"Interesting." Beryl pursed her lips. "I read somewhere that men who like Maryanne are the type who someday want to settle down, and that the ones who like Ginger--" Are only looking for someone to sleep with, is what the article had said, but of course, Beryl couldn't say that in front of Dominic and Duncan. "--well, aren't." A lame finish, but she figured Terry would get the gist.

He shrugged. "I liked her legs and her breathy voice."

Beryl rolled her eyes. "Naturally."

"Shhh," Duncan said, "it's back on."

After the program, Beryl sent the boys upstairs to put on their pajamas. They grumbled and griped, but then they bid Terry goodnight and did as they were told.

"I'll be up in a minute," she said.

Terry glanced up the stairs to make sure the boys weren't

lingering. He then took Beryl's hand and kissed her palm. "Thank you for inviting me to go this evening. I enjoyed it."

"Actually, Duncan invited you...but I enjoyed it, too."

"Can we do it again...say, Friday?" With another glance at the stairs, he circled her palm with his tongue.

She drew a quick breath. "Terry. We can't."

"I'm not asking you for anything more than what we had tonight...boys included."

"We can't," she repeated.

"Why the hell not?"

"Just...because." *Because you terrify me* was too honest to admit even to herself.

On Wednesday morning, the first thing Beryl said to Raife when she sat down in the makeup chair was, "Get this."

He grinned. "Sounds juicy. Are you finally gonna tell me what didn't happen this past weekend?"

Beryl rolled her eyes and sighed. "Not everything is about sex, Raife."

"I didn't say it was. Hmmm...more didn't happen this weekend than I thought."

She clamped her lips together and closed her eyes as he applied her blush.

"Come on," he said, when he could no longer endure the suspense. "Tell me."

Her eyes flew open and she leaned forward. "Okay. Yesterday I ran down to the basement and grabbed the file on Ron's and August's estate, and--"

"You actually found something down there?"

"Yes, Martha Stewart, I did. As I was saying, I took the estate information to work with me. It was a slow morning, and the dragon lady wasn't there--she had a doctor's appointment--so I went over it line by line."

"And what did you find, Nancy Drew?"

"We're sure doing a lot of name calling today, aren't we?"

"Yes." Raife stood back and looked at his handiwork thus far. "Close your eyes so I can give you that sexy smoky eye."

Beryl did as he instructed. "Anyway, I think Bob March is bilking the estates out of extra money."

"How do you figure?"

"Well, Ron's and August's legal expenses were exorbitant." She opened her eyes. "Plus, in Tennessee, an executor is only allowed to charge five percent of the personal property value. March charged twelve."

"Hmmm. Close your eyes again, babe."

Not being able to maintain eye contact made it more difficult to talk, but at least her hands weren't tied. As long as she could gesture her points home, she could talk. "Going on my theory, I looked up some other estates we've audited on the computer, and guess what?"

"Big legal bills?"

"You got it." She reopened her eyes. "With small estates, the bulk of it went to pay the funeral bills, and after March took his part, there was little, if any, left over for the families."

Raife shook his head. "Funerals are costly, Beryl. I'm sure that with smaller estates, it does take the majority of the money to pay the funeral expenses."

"I agree. But you're missing my point. In a case like that, the IRS would claim his executor's fees to be excessive and disallow it…not to mention the legal fees. In a small estate, with an uncontested will, there shouldn't be that great a need for legal services."

Raife turned the corners of his mouth down pensively. "You might have something then. But what can you do about it?"

"Since fraud is involved, I can get the IRS to reopen those cases that somehow slipped through the cracks. If found guilty, March would have to give back his fees in excess of what the IRS would allow and pay a fraud penalty and interest on the money he illegally gained. Plus, he could be disbarred, and he could go to jail."

"Let's get moving, people!" Joe called. "We have five minutes!"

Raife put the finishing touches to The Flame, and she raced onto the set. In today's first scene, she had to be lowered down through the ceiling of a jewelry store in order to catch the Gemstones in the act. She climbed a ladder, and took hold of the rope ready to anchor her legs and hands around it more securely when Joe gave the cue.

While the Gemstones laughed wickedly and filled laundry sacks with costume jewelry, Beryl watched Joe. When he pointed an index finger at her, she stepped off the ladder. But, rather than being eased down into the "jewelry store," Beryl plunged to the floor.

"Cut!" Joe yelled, rushing to Beryl's side as fast as his bulky form would allow. "What happened here? Beryl, you all right?"

"Uh, yeah...yeah, I'm okay." Her grimace belied her words.

"Where'd you hit?"

"I landed on my feet. It jolted me, that's all." She tried to sit up, but was still shaky. "Look, I know we're on dead air time right now. Let's get back on the air, let the Gemstones gloat about how The Flame fell, and we'll pick this back up tomorrow. We have enough here to finish out the show."

Joe nodded. "Okay, but you lie still. We're gonna have to wing it, girls." He backed away from the set. "Three...two...one. Let's roll!"

"Look, Opal," said a leggy blond in a green jumpsuit. "We have company."

"Yeah, Jade, I see that." Opal wore an iridescent white suit and a long white wig.

Ruby, a brunette in red, sauntered over to The Flame and stared down at her smugly. "Glad you could drop in, sweetie, but we really have to run."

As soon as the shoot was over, the saccharine trio gathered around Beryl to express their concern and to assure her that they were "just acting."

"I know," Beryl said with a feeble smile. She attempted to sit up, but Joe demanded that she lie still.

"I've had Raife call 9-1-1," he said. "You don't know that you've not broke your back or something."

Gee, thanks for the reassurance, Joe.

"They're on their way," Raife said, his head suddenly appearing beside Joe's.

"But I need to call work," Beryl protested.

"Done," Raife said.

"Did you tell them I'd be late?"

"No, I told them you'd be absent."

Beryl sighed. "I still need to call Mama. If she gets wind of this some other way--"

"I took care of that, too," Raife said. "She said to tell you she'll go by the schools and get Duncan and Dominic, and they'll meet you at the emergency room."

"There's no need for that," Beryl said with an exasperated huff.

"She was afraid some of the other kids saw it and would tell the boys wild stories," Raife said. "She didn't want them to be scared."

"No, I don't either." She closed her eyes, willing herself not to wince at the pain in her right leg. "That was good thinking. I'll have to tell her that."

"You're awfully pale, babe," Raife said, squatting beside her and smoothing the hair off her forehead. "I'm so sorry about this."

"It's not your fault," Beryl said, opening her eyes.

"That's debatable," Joe said, glaring at Raife. "We'll discuss it later."

"Is there anything I can get you?"

Beryl followed the nasal voice to Jade, a/k/a Irma Jenkins, secretary to the comptroller.

"No," Beryl said. "Thank you."

Jade popped her gum. "Well, lemme know if there's anything I can do." She turned and tripped over Beryl's hurt leg. "Oops. Sorry."

B eryl hobbled to the sofa and lay down, placing her crutches on the floor beside her. It was a comfort to be at home at last.

"Can you believe all this nonsense took over three and a half hours, and they never even did anything?" she asked.

"I know it seems that way, honey," Molly said, slipping a cushion beneath Beryl's right foot, "but at least we know nothing's broken. Do you want to go upstairs and put on something...well, less restricting?"

"In a minute, Mama." Beryl looked down at the yellow catsuit. It certainly wasn't the garment of choice right now--though she had to admit it had garnered her an unusual amount of attention in the emergency room (she staunchly refused to believe, however, that she was causing that old man to have a heart attack)--but she wasn't up to navigating the stairs yet.

Still wide-eyed and anxious, Dominic hovered near Beryl's head saying nothing...doing nothing...simply watching. Waiting to see what was happening and how it would affect him, Beryl supposed. Wondering if she would have to "go away for a while," too. It wrenched her heart to see him so concerned...so afraid.

"Come here," she told him, outstretching her arms.

He took a tentative step around to the front of the sofa.

"Give me a bear hug, Boo Diddle Dumplin'!"

"It won't hurt you?" he asked.

"It'll hurt my feelings if you don't."

He hugged her as if she was a frail little bird, but Beryl would take what she could get.

Duncan stood leaning over the other end of the sofa. "Do you need anything, Aunt B?"

Beryl smiled. "I could get used to this, guys. I really could. Hmmm…. Let me think. Do I need anything?"

"Uh-oh," Duncan said, rolling his dark eyes at Dominic. "She's got that look."

Dominic shook his little head solemnly.

"Let's start with a hot fudge sundae…with peanut butter and--"

"Peanut butter!" Duncan grimaced and stuck out his tongue.

"Ever tried it?"

He shook his head.

"Then don't knock it. You guys ask for some pretty weird stuff when you're sick, too, you know." She cocked her head. "And I want a new race game and my teddy bear and--"

"You not got a teddy bear, Aunt B-B Head," Dominic chided with a grin.

"I don't? Well, then, can I snuggle with Harvey?"

"You'll give him back when you're done?"

"Of course. Or I could just snuggle you instead!" She reached to tickle him, and he scooted out of the way giggling.

The doorbell rang. Duncan and Dominic were still laughing as they raced to open the door.

Beryl closed her eyes and put the back of her hand to her forehead. "Let in my adoring fans, guys! Perhaps one will be a strong, handsome gentleman who I can impose upon to carry me up yon stairs!" She added that last part with the certainty that her guest would be Raife, especially as he hadn't put in an appearance at the hospital.

"Will I do?"

Terry. Beryl's eyes snapped open and she struggled to sit up.

He took her arm. "Here. Let me help."

"What're you doing here?"

"Just came to check on the patient…who apparently needs assistance getting up 'yon stairs.'" He started to place his arms beneath her knees and shoulders.

"No, no, no," she said quickly. "That's fine. Actually, I thought you were someone else."

"Still, you need to go upstairs, and I can take you."

"Good idea," Molly said, emerging from the kitchen. "You two go on upstairs so Beryl can change."

"Mama--"

"Boys, come on in here and get your lunch. Terry, yours and Beryl's will be waiting when you get back downstairs."

"Why, thank you," he said, and swept Beryl into his arms as if she had no say in the matter whatsoever...which--obviously--she didn't.

At the top of the stairs, his request for directions was met by:

"What are you doing here, Terry?"

"I told you, I came to see how you are. That was a nasty fall this morning. Naturally, I thought it was part of the show until--"

"Thought it was part of the show? You mean, you watched the show?"

He shifted her in his arms. "You're getting heavy. Do you want me to set you down right here, or do you want to tell me where your room is?"

"Here is fine."

Terry narrowed his eyes. "Why do you have to be so damned impossible?" He strode down the hall and saw that those bedrooms obviously belonged to the boys. He didn't think Beryl would have race cars and construction sets strewn about her floor.

He turned, went the opposite way, located her room, and unceremoniously dropped Beryl on her antique canopy bed. Yes, this frilly room with its lacy bedspread, lacy curtains, and cutesy doo-dads was definitely hers.

"Thank you," she said.

He stood staring at her, his eyes blazing like blue topaz.

"I said, 'thank you,'" she repeated.

"Oh, so now I'm being dismissed?"

"Unless you want to tell me what you were doing watching a stupid children's show this morning."

"It's not stup--" He lifted his hands dismissively before placing them on his trim waist.

Beryl tried not to think about what a gorgeous man he was...tried not to notice how his navy slacks fit just so...tried to ignore how his white oxford accented the firm muscles in his chest and arms…tried not to remember how wonderful it had felt to kiss him and hold him and run her hands over his body and have him run his hands over her body. She closed her eyes.

"Listen," he said, "let's get what you need and get back downstairs."

"I can manage."

"Like hell. Why won't you let me help you?"

"Why do you want to?"

"Who knows? But I'm going to."

"What is this? A balm for your guilty conscience?"

"Guilty conscience over what?"

"Over this weekend!"

"You told me that was--" He held up his fingers and wiggled them to indicate quotation marks. "--'no biggie.'"

"And it wasn't. So you shouldn't have a guilty conscience, should you?"

"I don't have!"

"Fine!"

"Fine!"

"Will you two kids keep it down?" Molly called from the bottom of the stairs. "Don't make me come up there," she added with a chuckle.

Terry and Beryl exchanged glares.

"Truce?" Terry asked.

Beryl lifted one shoulder apathetically.

"Now, how can I help?" Terry asked.

"If you'll please open my closet door, I'll see what I'd like to wear."

Terry went to the closet and opened the door with a flourish. "See anything you like?"

Beryl wisely let that pass without the comment she'd like to have made. "Royal blue chenille sweater and black leggings."

Terry got the garments out of the closet and handed them to Beryl. "Anything else?"

"I'll need socks."

Terry felt of Beryl's bare feet, being careful of the right one, which was tightly wrapped from the middle of the foot to the shin. "I guess so. These poor little things are like ice."

"I'll need a bra and panties. I don't wear any with this."

Terry went to the chest of drawers. "In here?"

Beryl nodded. "Top drawer."

Terry opened the drawer and was immediately tantalized by the scent of peaches. He closed his eyes and took a deep breath.

"Mr. Goodson, are you smelling my underwear?"

He opened his eyes and frowned at her. "I got a whiff of peaches when I opened the drawer!"

"It's a sachet. Could you hand me the black lace set please?"

"Gladly."

"Then, if you'll unzip me, I can manage the rest."

"All right." He moved behind her and she held up her hair. He slowly unzipped the catsuit.

Beryl resisted the urge to lean back against him. She couldn't let him see how affected she was by him. She stiffened as she felt his lips against the back of her neck. They were starting to slide down her back. She hastily dropped her hair on his face.

"I'll be ready to go back downstairs in a jif," she said.

Terry nodded. "I'll wait outside the door."

"Thanks." She winked to underscore how unmoved she was.

As soon as Terry got outside the room, she fanned herself with both hands.

"Will you be in trouble for leavin' school early, Mr. Goodson?" Duncan asked as Terry helped Beryl into her chair.

"No. After your grandma came and picked you up, I called and asked them to send over a substitute for this afternoon's classes." He took the vacant chair to Beryl's left. "I wanted to come by and see if you guys needed anything...see how your aunt was doing."

"We appreciate your concern," Molly said warmly. She looked around the table. "Don't we?"

Beryl and the boys murmured their agreement.

As the boys watched the oven in parted lips anticipation of the timer's announcement that the pan of brownies had finished baking, Terry and Beryl devoured still-warm croissants stuffed with homemade chicken salad.

"Mama, these are delicious," Beryl said. "I hadn't realized how hungry I was."

"Yes," Terry said. "They're fabulous."

"You two haven't tasted anything yet," Molly said.

As if on cue, the timer announced that the brownies were ready.

Molly stood and put on oven mitts. As she took the pan out of the oven, she smiled impishly at Beryl and Terry. "Never leave the table before the meal is finished."

She sat the pan on a trivet, closed the oven door and turned off the oven. "If you exercise a little restraint...a little self-control...you'll realize that what you've sampled so far is only the beginning of the wonderful fare you can have if you're willing to be patient and give yourself some breathing room." She opened a cabinet and removed five glass bowls. "Because--if you want it--the best is yet to come."

"I want it, Grandma!" Duncan shouted.

"Me, too! Me, too!" Dominic chirped.

Molly chuckled as she retrieved spoons and a cake server. "Everyone does, my sweethearts, if they're honest with themselves." She took a half-gallon of vanilla ice cream from the freezer and put a small jar of fudge sauce in the microwave. "You'll be wanting peanut butter with yours, Beryl?"

"Of course, Mama." Beryl knew precisely where the old gal had been going with her metaphor.

"I'll try that, too, please," Terry said.

Within minutes, before each of them sat a dish overflowing with a warm brownie, two scoops of ice cream, warm fudge sauce, whipped cream, and--on two--peanut butter. Beryl eagerly picked up her spoon and dove into the rich concoction. When she tasted it, she moaned in ecstasy.

Terry's spoon clattered to the floor.

9

After Molly and the boys had put the dishes in the dishwasher and cleaned up the kitchen, Molly announced that they were going over to check on Ralph and to "get a few things" so she could stay there with Beryl tonight.

"Now, Mama, you don't have to do that," Beryl protested. "What about Daddy?"

"He'll be fine. I've already spoken with Bill, and he doesn't mind using the guest room tonight."

"He's been using it a lot lately."

"Not that much." Molly shrugged. "Besides, he likes my cooking."

"Who doesn't?" Duncan asked.

"You are an excellent cook, Mrs. Madison," Terry said.

"Molly, please. I like to be on a first-name basis with someone before I ask him a favor."

"Mama," Beryl began, her brows drawn in a ferocious grimace that her mother completely ignored.

"What is it?" Terry asked.

"Would you mind staying with our patient until we return?"

"Not at all."

"I don't need a babysitter," Beryl protested.

"Uh-huh," Dominic said. "You might fall and get hurt again."

That, of course, was Beryl's undoing. She graciously thanked Terry for agreeing to stay until her mother and the boys returned.

"Actually, I am glad for the opportunity to talk with you alone,"

Beryl said, stretching out on the sofa.

Terry raised his brows and pulled his chair closer. "What's on your mind?"

"Ever since doing your audit, I've been thinking about my sister's and her husband's estate." She went on to explain her observations and conclusions.

"Makes sense," Terry said, sitting back in his chair. "But what're we gonna do?"

"I don't know. I don't want to dredge up anything painful for Mama, Duncan and Dominic. But how can I let this keep going on?"

Terry clasped his hands behind his head. "I'm sorry I dumped all that mess on you that day."

"You didn't know Bob March had handled August's and Ron's estate."

"I know, but still--" He shook his head. "I don't want anything painful dredged up for you or your family either."

"I just wonder if there is something I could do without it affecting them."

"How about without it affecting you?"

"But it already has affected me, Terry. Now I don't know how to let it go, but I don't know how to do anything about it, either."

He leaned his head back against the cradle of his hands and stared up at the ceiling. "If we could do it quietly...keep it out of the media...."

"A scam like that? No way."

"Okay, let's say it did get in the media. Do the boys watch the local news?"

"No."

"And I know they don't read the newspaper."

"Of course not."

"So, it would be fairly simple for us to shield Duncan and Dominic. As for your mother..." He lowered his head back to Beryl's eye level. "I think that if we take this to the authorities, we need to tell her before it goes public."

Beryl nodded while digesting his suggestion.

"She strikes me as a strong woman," he continued. "I think it would be painful for her, but I think she'd rather we pursue this rather than sweep it under the rug." He took Beryl's hand. "Think about it. How does Molly feel about any injustices suffered by her children?"

Beryl snorted. "There's no injustice greater...except maybe an injustice to Duncan and Dominic."

"Then you have your answer." He caressed her hand with his thumb. "Now I'd like a couple of answers of my own."

"Okay." She kept her voice light, but she avoided his eyes.

"Look at me."

She dragged her eyes up to his.

He moved his face close to hers. "Do you want me to kiss you?"

Beryl lowered her eyes.

"Huh-uh," Terry said. "I want an answer--an honest answer. And I want you to look me in the eye when you give me that answer."

Beryl tightened her lips and lifted her eyes, but when she saw the tenderness in Terry's eyes, her resolve went out the window. She placed her free hand behind his head and pulled his head down to hers. Beryl had never felt anything as strong as her longing for this man...except the love of her nephews.

Terry ended their kiss and released Beryl's hand when the doorbell rang.

"That's probably Raife," Beryl said. "Would you please let him in?"

"Of course...but remember, I still have some unanswered questions."

Raife was at the door, but so was James Appleton with a potted plant. As the men stepped into the living room, James gazed around the room.

"You have a nice home, Beryl."

"Thank you...and thank you for the plant...though you really shouldn't have after the bouquet you sent Monday."

"Ah, but this is of the genus *Eupatorium*," James said. "It's called boneset because it's supposed to have healing properties. And while I don't know whether that's true or not--I'm generally not given to myths and lore--I thought it an appropriate plant to bring just in case." He gave her his toothpaste commercial smile, and she nodded.

"Thanks."

"And thanks so much for dropping in to check on our girl," Raife said. "So sorry you two can't stay, but it's obvious Beryl needs her rest, and I'm sure you guys have things to do."

"But I just got here," James said.

"We certainly do appreciate your thoughtfulness and concern," Raife said, reopening the door Terry had just closed. "Perhaps we can have you over for dinner after Beryl is on the mend."

"'We,'" James echoed. "I didn't realize that you...that Beryl...." He gave Beryl a playground-whiner look. "But I...I didn't think you were involved with anyone."

Beryl opened her mouth to reply without quite knowing what to say. While she didn't want James to get the wrong impression, she wasn't sure she wanted him to have the right one either.

Raife saved her from having to say anything at all. "Beryl brightens my every morning. I'm blessed to have her in my life." He took the boneset James was still holding, sat it on the coffee table, and gently but firmly propelled James out the door. "Goodbye, gentlemen."

"Beryl," Terry said, "if you need me, you have my number."

"Yes, I do. Thank you."

With a nod at Raife, Terry followed James out the door.

"You got them out of here like they were termites at a house warming," Beryl said. "And, by the way, I'm blessed to have you in my life, too. That was a sweet thing for you to say. Now, what's up?"

"I saw that Molly's car wasn't here, and I need to talk with you alone." He sat down in the chair Terry had vacated when the doorbell rang. "Joe's threatening to fire me."

"Why?"

"He thinks I'm becoming too negligent with the props. First the thing with the banana and now this morning's mishap. He thinks it was my fault you fell today."

"What happened? What did cause me to fall?"

Raife sighed and raked his hands through his hair. "I don't know. I thought everything was fine. You know I wouldn't risk your being hurt."

"What happened?" Beryl repeated.

"I guess I didn't have the rope tight enough. When you pulled on it, it was supposed to have been taut so you could swing out over the set and lower yourself down easily. Instead, when you pulled on it, the spool gave way, unreeled the rope too fast, and down you went."

Beryl looked down at her swollen ankle. She didn't doubt that it had been a miscalculation. Yet, it was a miscalculation that was now causing her a lot of pain...and it could've been worse.

"I'm so sorry," Raife said.

"I know." Beryl looked back at him. "Maybe Joe should get another prop man."

Raife gaped at her. "You agree that he should fire me?"

"No! I just think you have too much to do. I think he should let you do what you do best--hair, makeup, costumes, voiceovers--and hire someone else to do the props."

"But he won't do that."

"He'll have to. He can't find another prop man who can do what you can with hair and makeup."

"How do you know?"

"I know."

"You're really upset with me, aren't you?"

Beryl expelled a long breath. "I'm not upset with you. It's just that--"

"You think I was negligent."

"You were, Raife." She spread her hands. "I'm not saying it's all your fault--Joe is as much to blame as anybody, and I'll tell him that. You're pulled in too many directions at the station. You've said that before yourself."

"I know, but I love my job. I don't want to lose it."

Beryl placed her hand on his forearm. "You won't."

"I hope not." He stood and tramped to the door. He turned and looked back at her. Then with a sigh and a shake of his head, he was gone.

Beryl lugged herself up the stairs to the bathroom and ran herself a hot bath. She took along her cell phone in case Molly should call.

What had transpired between her and Raife tonight was the closest thing to an argument they'd ever had. She realized he loved his job. But she also realized that he had too many responsibilities to give each one the care he should. He simply couldn't. It was impossible.

Trying to ignore the throbbing in her leg, she lowered herself into the bathtub. No sooner than she had, the phone rang.

"Hello?"

"Beryl, you sound like you're in a canyon," Terry said. "Where are you?"

"I'm in the bathtub."

"Don't remind me of missed opportunities."

"Excuse me?"

"Nothing. Are you alone?"

She scoffed. "No, the Tennessee Titans are in here with me. Excuse me, could one of you defensive linemen hand me the soap?"

"Ha, ha. I meant, is Raife still there?"

"No."

"How'd you get up the stairs?"

She scoffed again. "What is this, an inquisition? I took my little crutches and climbed one stair at a time."

"I called to see if you're okay."

"I'm in about the same shape as I was when you saw me a few minutes ago, except now I'm in water."

"Listen, smart ass, I was driving home when I remembered that Raife is your prop man."

"And?"

"And he was in an awfully big hurry to get you to himself."

"He wanted to talk to me about the accident."

"What did he come up with?"

"The truth. Something happened with the reel the rope was wound around."

"Whose fault was the accident, Beryl?"

"Technically, it was Raife's, but--"

"Didn't you tell me Bob March owns an interest in the station?"

"Yes. You're really playing hopscotch with the twenty questions, aren't you?"

"No, actually, I'm not. I'm trying to ask you whether or not March could've put Raife up to rigging the rope to let you fall."

"Terry! I can't believe you'd accuse Raife of doing such a thing!"

"I'm not accusing anyone of anything. I'm only speculating. I don't know Raife like you do."

"No, you don't. Raife is one of my best friends. I certainly don't think he'd accept hit man duty."

"I'm not saying he was trying to kill you, only scare you."

"Why would he? How would Bob March even know I've been checking up on him?"

"I don't know. How would he, Beryl?" He paused. "Besides me, who have you told?"

She was silent.

"Who, Beryl?"

"Raife."

"It's not my intention to upset you, sweetheart, only to protect you. I just want you to be careful, okay?"

"How can I not be careful? My mommy's taking me to work tomorrow."

"You're going to work tomorrow? At the station? How do you think--"

"No, not at the station," she interrupted. "At the IRS. I'm only part-time and I can't afford to miss a day. I don't have sick days."

"The station should be reimbursing you for the days you miss at both jobs, but let's not get into that tonight. I'll take you to work in the morning. Your mom will have plenty to do getting the boys to school and getting back home to see to your dad."

"Thank you for your generous offer, but--"

"No 'buts'. It's right on my way."

"It is not."

"Practically."

"You need to be at work earlier than I do."

"Says who?"

"Don't teachers have bus duty and all that?"

"Damn. I am supposed to do bus duty tomorrow morning. But, that's okay," he said, before she could speak. "I'll call Pam Robbins. She'll sub for me. She owes me one."

Pam Robbins a/k/a The Bimbo.... "Maybe. But if you drive me to work tomorrow, then I'll owe you one."

Terry chuckled. "Interesting. I think I like having you beholden to me."

"Then enjoy it for the short time I will be. I detest owing anything to anyone, so why don't I make dinner for you tomorrow night to even the score?"

"Not the most gracious invitation I've ever had, but I accept. I'm looking forward to sampling your culinary delights."

B eryl had a difficult time concentrating that night. Not because of Terry's suspicions about Raife...not even because of his apparent misconception about her cooking prowess...but because of the way he mentioned missed opportunities...referred to how "we" were going to handle the situation with Bob March ...insisted on taking her to work tomorrow morning...carried her up and down the stairs...dropped his spoon.

"Okay," Molly said, after the boys had gone to bed, "you've been preoccupied all evening. What's up?"

Beryl shook her head. "Nothing really."

"Terry?"

She nodded.

"Have you slept together?"

"No, Mama. Why do you always think that's what's on my mind when I mention Terry?"

"Because if--"

"I know, I know. But no, Mama, we haven't. You should know I wouldn't do anything with the boys here."

"Sorry." Molly looked hurt by her daughter's admonition. "But they weren't here this afternoon."

"As a matter of fact, I didn't even let him kiss me goodnight last night."

"Last night?"

"Yes, he went to dinner with the boys and me."

"So you two are dating then?"

"No...it wasn't a date exactly. He merely happened to be here, and Duncan and I were getting ready to leave to pick up Dominic and go to dinner, and Duncan invited Terry along, and..."

"Sounds like a date to me."

"Well, it wasn't. He's a confirmed bachelor, Mama. He might be interested in fooling around a little, but he isn't interested in a relationship."

"Then get him interested."

Beryl looked at her mother as if she was reading the suggestion out of a sleazy tabloid opposite the article "How to Increase Your Bust Two Cup Sizes Overnight--Without Surgery!"

"And just how do I do that?" she asked.

Something in Molly's knowing grin caused Beryl to lean forward as if her mother were about to tell her all the secrets of the universe.

10

I t was raining the next morning. Terry drove to Beryl's house lulled into an almost hypnotic reflection by the swish-swish of the windshield wipers. Pam would be even more thrilled than she was last night about taking his bus duty this morning seeing how the rain was coming down.

Why couldn't he simply have a fling with Pam? She wanted it. He'd wanted it…until he'd looked into those big green eyes of Beryl Madison. With Pam it would've been unencumbered. They could've each taken what they'd wanted and walked away. No strings. No visions of picket fences and woolly dogs. No turning on the television as soon as he got out of bed weekday mornings in order to watch a silly kids' show just so he could see her.

What was the matter with him? He'd never been such a sap before.

As the BMW glided into Beryl's driveway, Beryl stepped out onto the porch. Seeing that she intended on maneuvering herself, her briefcase, her umbrella, and her crutches off the porch and to the car by herself, Terry slammed the gearshift into park and, leaving the car door open, rushed to help her.

"Are you nuts?" he asked.

"I don't know," she said with mock earnestness. "As I recall, you're the psychoanalyst. Am I nuts? Maybe you can analyze me on the way to the office and find out."

Shaking his head, he took her briefcase and placed it under his arm. He took hold of the umbrella she carried and held it over her as he put a steadying hand on her left arm. He didn't bother to try to share the umbrella--his jog to the porch had left him drenched.

He deposited Beryl and her briefcase into the car, shook out the umbrella and put it in the back before resuming his now-damp seat behind the wheel.

"You look sexy wet," Beryl said. "Too bad we have to go to work."

Or what? he wanted to ask. Are you playing with me or are you serious? If you're serious and we make love...how could I ever walk away from you?

A little voice inside reminded him that he hadn't quite walked away after just *wanting* to make love to her.

"Let me be the first to tell you," he said, hoping that making conversation would help chase away that little voice, "that you look exquisite this morning."

And she did. A double-breasted royal blue suit brought out the fire in both her hair and her eyes. Though he loved seeing her legs, she looked elegant in the slacks and flats she had worn to camouflage her injury.

"By the look in those baby blues," Beryl said, "I'll give you a dime for your thoughts."

He grinned. "I'll bet you would."

"So?"

He laughed. "I'm not that cheap, sweetheart."

"All right then. I'll really make it worth your while. Give me your thoughts, and I'll give you something of equal value when we get to my office."

"Sounds interesting."

"Extremely. Are your thoughts as interesting as my offer?"

"Maybe." He cast her a sidelong glance. "You confided to me yesterday that you don't wear undergarments with your Flame costume."

"Right."

"What do you wear under your business suits, Madame Auditor?"

Beryl's response to his question was a husky, throaty laugh.

"So?"

"Pink lace."

"With the faint scent of peaches, I'm sure."

She laughed again. "You should know."

He reminded her of her offer of "something of equal value" in exchange for his thoughts as he escorted her into her office.

"Oh, yeah, I did, didn't I? Push the door up, please."

He did so, and Beryl dropped her crutches and put her arms around his neck. She pulled his mouth down to hers and gave him a kiss that nearly dried his clothes.

A s soon as Terry left Beryl's office, Clark Samuels burst in…at least, it was "bursting" for Clark.

"Thank God you are alive!" he said, arms akimbo like some kind of odd, little balding bird attempting flight after being booted from the nest.

"Yes," Beryl agreed. "I…I am grateful."

"Yesterday morning, I was watching The Flame, and--"

Do any children watch that show? Beryl wondered.

"--when you crashed to the floor, and then when there was that dead air time, I couldn't help myself." He splayed his hands across his chest. "I yelled, 'Damn those Gemstones! Damn them!' Mother was so outraged at my foul language that she nearly had another of those spells of hers." His hands fluttered toward the ceiling. "Naturally, I thought the fall was just part of the plot--you know, like when Wild Man tosses you into a pit or something--until Nancy said you wouldn't be in because you'd been injured on 'that silly T. V. thing she does'. Her words, not mine, mind you."

"Of course."

"I think it's thrilling myself," Clark continued, wagging his brows, "to have an office right across the hall from The Flame herself." He lowered his voice to a whisper. "I even bought one of your coloring books. I'd only had the chance to fill in the first couple of pages, though, before Mother found it, said it was vile, and tossed it into the garbage pail." His thin lips tightened. "I'd have retrieved it, but just after she threw it in, she choked on a sip of vegetable juice and spit up right on my book."

"Really."

"I'm afraid so. Of course, Mother blamed that on the book, too. She said it was practically pornography and that when she happened upon me stroking your body with a yellow crayon that was little more than a phallic symbol, she nearly had an apoplexy."

Beryl's eyes widened as she stifled the giggle that bubbled up inside her. "I'm sorry to hear that, Clark. I actually have a copy of the latest coloring book in my briefcase. I'd love for you to have it, but I'd hate to be the cause of more friction between you and your mother."

"Oh! Oh, no!" A flush spread across Clark's usually pasty face. "It wouldn't cause any trouble at all. I could keep it here...in my desk...hidden...locked."

"Are you sure?" she asked.

"Oh, positive! Positive!"

"Well, in that case, would you hand me my briefcase, please?"

Clark complied with her request and only tripped over one chair in the process.

Beryl opened the briefcase and extracted the book. Before she handed it to him, he insisted that she autograph it.

Beryl inscribed, "Hugs and Kisses, The Flame," inside a little fire. She glanced up, saw the open exhilaration on his face, and thought, *What the heck?* She raised the book to her lips and pressed an open-mouthed kiss on it, leaving a coral lip print.

"Ooooh!" Clark exclaimed. "I can hardly wait until lunch so I can go out and buy a 64-pack of crayons with a sharpener." Clutching the thin coloring book, he scurried to the door, opened it, banged his forehead with it, oomphed, rubbed his forehead, and left.

"Oh, wait," he said, opening the door back up. "I forgot to tell you. I got you a mum as a get-well gift, but I was so allergic that I had to put it on the back porch. Mother has allergies, too, you know, so I couldn't very well bring it inside." He sighed. "To make a long story short, the neighbor's cat knocked it off the porch railing." He lowered his head. "It's gone."

"I'm sorry to hear that," Beryl said. "It is the thought that counts, though, Clark."

"I'm glad you feel that way. Perhaps I can frame one of your completed pictures, and--"

Beryl held up her hands. "Oh, no...no, thanks, Clark." She began riffling through papers on her desk. "I'd better get started on all this work now."

"Okay." He left again, this time stumping his toe and practically falling into his office before scrambling back to close her door. "Sorry."

Beryl blew out a breath. Now...what to do first....

Before she could review the work to prioritize it, however, the phone rang. Beryl could see it was going to be one of those days.

"Yes?" she answered a tad impatiently.

"Beryl, it's Joe. How're you feeling, hon?"

"I'm doing all right, Joe. Are we resuming production tomorrow morning?"

"If you're up to it. Are you?"

"I think so. I'm not up to wearing the boots, but if the camera guys will shoot me from the waist up, we should be fine."

"All right. I'll get a writer on it and drop a script by to you this evening." He paused. "Spoke to Raife yesterday."

"He told me you did." Beryl didn't elaborate, waiting to see where Joe was headed.

"He made a big mistake yesterday morning."

Joe let the statement hang, making Beryl feel she had to respond somehow. She decided to speak her mind.

"I think Raife has too many responsibilities to do them all adequately."

"I think I might let him go."

"He's a wonderful hair and makeup man. You know you couldn't find a better one. Plus, there's no one who could do the costumes and voiceovers as well. Raife is the voice of *The Flame*."

Silence.

"I think the prop person should be a separate job," Beryl continued.

"Beryl, you know the station can't afford to hire someone else."

"How about an intern? There are too many colleges around here for there not to be at least one or two students who need a media internship."

Joe was again silent, and Beryl could picture him puffing out his chubby cheeks the way he always did when he was thinking. He finally responded.

"Not a bad idea, kid. I'll look into it."

The rest of the day passed pretty much without incident. Nancy made the snide comment that people who acted their age and didn't run about in silly costumes didn't have to worry about the hazards of unnecessary risks; and Clark ran across the hall to Beryl's office after lunch with his coloring book slipped into a file folder so he could show her his lunch-hour masterpiece. Other than that, the day was business as usual. Come to think of it, that kinda was business as usual for Beryl.

She was relieved when she saw Molly's dark blue Explorer wheel into the parking lot. Duncan's little dark head was barely visible even with his booster seat on the passenger side, and Dominic's bobbed excitedly from his car seat in the back.

Beryl grabbed her briefcase, stuck it under her arm and reached for her crutches. The briefcase crashed to the floor. She'd forgotten that she'd had Terry's assistance this morning.

A faint smile touched her lips as she remembered the kiss she'd given him. She hadn't forgotten that. She was playing with fire. She knew better than to toy with a man like Terry. Not even The Flame could play with that kind of explosive without getting burned...but she was unfortunately like the proverbial moth.

She locked the briefcase and pushed it up under her desk. She didn't need to take it home this evening, and it certainly wasn't worth the trouble to ask Molly to come back in and get it.

She made her way out to the parking lot, and both Molly and Duncan hurried out of the car to offer their assistance.

"Gee, thanks," Beryl said, smiling broadly at her helpers and waving to Dominic. "I feel like a celebrity."

"You are to us, Aunt B."

Molly winked and helped Beryl into the car.

Beryl allowed Duncan to stay where he was, and she slid into the backseat beside Dominic. "I'm gonna sit back here and love on this handsome guy."

Apparently, the proposition appealed to Dominic. He held out his arms and puckered his lips.

"I started to lay out something for dinner," Molly said, as she began navigating the Explorer out of the parking lot, "but I remembered Raife usually comes over and cooks on Thursday."

"Not tonight," Beryl said. "He called this afternoon and told me something had come up. But, that's okay, I was planning on cooking dinner myself anyway."

"You were?" Molly asked. Her questioning eyes met Beryl's in the rearview.

"But why?" Duncan asked.

Beryl shrugged. "I'm making dinner for Mr. Goodson tonight to repay him for driving me to work this morning."

"Did he nearly wreck ya or somethin'?" Duncan asked.

"No." Beryl bit her bottom lip. "I think I've been making improvements in my cooking abilities...don't you guys?"

The boys looked down at their laps while Molly kept her eyes riveted to the road. It wasn't the answer Beryl had been hoping for. But that was okay. She'd show them.

The Flame never backed down from a challenge. *Wherever there is a wrong to be righted, an injustice to be overcome, an oppression to be liberated, an egg to be fried, or a burger to be grilled, The Flame will be there. She alone can scorch evil, char cruelty, sear tyranny, ignite fear in the hearts of even the coldest of criminals...and burn even Minute Rice®.*

No, no, no. She refused to let doubt be her downfall. She could make a good meal. After all, she'd already made one good meal this week...sort of... hadn't she?

"Do you mind stopping by the store, Mama?" she asked.

"Not at all, honey. Not at all." Though Molly's answer was as bright as fireworks on Independence Day, she staunchly refused to let her eyes stray toward the rearview.

In the store, the boys begged to go to the toy section.

"Will you be all right, dear?" Molly asked.

"I'll be fine. Go on with the boys so I can concentrate on what I'm doing please."

"Well, um..." Molly cleared her throat. "What...what do you plan on making, sweetie?"

"It'll be a surprise." Beryl dismissed her mother with a smile and took off in the direction of the produce. A glance over her shoulder assured her that Molly and the boys were on their way to the toy aisle.

If she remembered correctly, August used to make this Frenchy sounding beef stew called pot of something. It had meat and vegetables, and August had cooked it all together in a Dutch oven. How hard could that be?

Beryl scanned the bins of produce as she tried to recall all the ingredients August put in that beef stew concoction. Carrots, of course. Every beef stew had carrots. But August put some frou-frou veggies into hers to make it Frenchy and gourmet. She used parsnips instead of potatoes, for instance. Personally, Beryl preferred potatoes, but if she meant to impress Terry, she'd better go with the parsnips. Now, what else? Leeks, she thought, but hey, what are leeks except little onions? The onion bin was closer to her than the leek bin was, and her ankle was starting to throb. Beryl went with the onions.

Now to the meat department. Using the shopping cart like a walker, Beryl hurried to the meat freezer and grabbed the first slab of beef that looked stewable. She was making her way to the front of the store when Molly and the boys ventured out of the toy aisle.

"Got everything you need?" Molly asked, studying the contents of Beryl's cart from the corners of her eyes.

"Yep. This'll be a cinch."

Molly nodded. "Yes, well...I hope you don't mind, but I told the boys I'd get them each a storybook."

"That's fine, Mama. Thank you." She glanced down to see their selections. Duncan had a Superman book and Dominic held a Winnie the Pooh book. "Good choices, guys. Maybe Grandma will read them to you while I make dinner."

"Okay," Duncan said.

"Mine first?" Dominic asked.

"We'll see." Beryl spotted a checker with no one in her line. "Come on."

Molly went first, insisting that she buy the boys their books. Then, pointing out that Beryl was hardly able to do so herself, she took the things from Beryl's cart and put them on the conveyor. Now that she could peruse the dinner ingredients more openly, she asked, "I know it's supposed to be a surprise, but what are you planning to make, honey?"

"That beef stew...pot of—" She wrinkled her brow. "Pot of what? It has a French sounding name.... What is it, Mama?"

Molly's eyes widened. "*Pot-au-feu?* You're planning to make *pot-au-feu?*"

"Yeah. How hard can it be?"

"*Pot-au-feu* takes quite a while," Molly said. "Are you sure you'll have enough time?"

Beryl dismissed Molly's concerns with a flick of her wrist. "I'll brown the meat a little first and turn the stove on high. It'll be fine."

The checker announced the total, her eyes darting back and forth between the mother and daughter during their exchange.

Beryl paid the lady, smiled and repeated, "It'll be fine."

As soon as they got home, Molly ushered the boys into the den to read the new books, leaving Beryl alone in the kitchen to get the meal underway.

Beryl whistled a happy, wandering little tune as she took the Dutch oven out of the cabinet and placed it on the stove. She unwrapped the meat and placed it squarely into the center of the pot. Since she had only an hour and a half before Terry was to arrive, she turned the eye on high so that the meat would brown quickly. She watched it carefully so it wouldn't burn, and flipped it over often.

While the meat was browning, she let the hot water run so it would be plenty hot when she was ready to put some on the meat. She saw no point in making the stove work overtime.

Seeing that the meat was pretty well browned, Beryl took the Dutch oven over to the sink and let the hot water pour over the meat. The eye hissed like a coiled red snake as she returned the pot. Beryl quickly scraped the carrots and parsley and tossed them into the water whole. She cut off the outer layer of the onions and tossed them in as well. Now she was ready to let the stove and the pot do the rest of the work while she went upstairs and took a bath.

The warm water was wonderfully soothing to her sore ankle, so Beryl lay back in the tub to soak awhile. She wet her washcloth and placed it over her forehead.

Why was she working so hard to impress Terry Goodson? This morning, she'd flirted outrageously with him, and now she was trying to make him a gourmet dinner. He'd made it clear he was interested in pursuing a relationship with her—no, not really a relationship—sex. And while Beryl was certain it would be fabulous, mind blowing, life-altering sex, she wanted more than that. She didn't think Terry did. So now her mind was back to its original question– why was she trying so hard? Maybe she wanted him to regret "the one that got away." Or maybe she was foolish enough to think he'd fall in love with her. That's what Mama seemed to think.

She swiped the washcloth off her face and tossed it into the tub. She was being ridiculous. She was making dinner for a friend, that's all…a dinner that smelled pretty darn good, if she had to say so herself. And given the skepticism of her family, she probably would have to say so herself.

She bathed, got out of the tub and put on a curve-skimming, deep violet jersey dress. It had long sleeves, was ankle length and was very comfortable. Beryl had been told by more than one person that she looked great in this dress...but, of course, she put it on because it was so comfortable. Of course.

By the time she'd reapplied her makeup, slipped on a pair of black satin ballet slippers and eased downstairs, Terry was there.

"Hello," she said. "You're early."

"A little. Since your ankle is hurt and you had to work all day, I thought I'd come in time to see if there's anything I can help you do."

"No. Everything is under control."

"Dinner certainly smells great. What're we having?"

Beryl beamed at the compliment, glad that she didn't have to be the one who pointed out that dinner smelled good. At last, her cooking skills were going to be validated. "We're having *pot-au-feu*."

"French?"

"Hmm-hmm." She smiled at Molly and the boys who were giving their books their rapt attention. "I'd better go in and check on it."

"Shall I help you, honey?" Molly asked.

"Oh, no, just continue with your reading."

When she opened the lid to the Dutch oven, she gasped. The vegetables had turned to mush and the meat was coated in a greasy scum.

She grabbed a serving platter and a handful of paper towels. She placed half of the towels on the bottom of the platter, then skewered the meat and lifted it out of the pot. It slid off the meat fork and back into the oily broth splattering Beryl and her "comfortable" dress.

Grinding her teeth, she speared the meat once again and this time maneuvered it onto the platter. She covered the meat with the remaining paper towels. She snatched up a dishtowel and ran one end under cold water. She dabbed at the broth on her dress but only made the wet spots larger. She gave up and set the table.

"Is it done, Aunt B?" Duncan called. "We're hungry."

"Almost. I'll call you when it's ready." She managed to wipe the majority of the grease off the meat, gathered up the paper towels, and shoved them into the trash. She added the meat fork and a serving knife to the platter of meat and set it on the table. "Okay."

"It's ready?" Molly asked.

"Yes." *I think.*

"Looks good," Terry said, strolling into the kitchen ahead of Beryl's apprehensive family members.

"Is that it?" Duncan asked, sitting in his usual spot. "Just meat?"

Beryl smiled. "Well, of course not. We wouldn't have just meat." She went over to the pantry to see what she could serve with the meat. "We were going to have vegetables with it, but I didn't think you guys would like those—"

"Sure we would," Terry said.

She peeped around the pantry door. "No, you wouldn't. They're frou-frou vegetables. Nobody likes them. They just flavor the meat."

"Oh."

"We're having these with the meat." She held up the only bag of "vegetables" she could readily produce that were edible.

"Chips?" Molly asked.

"Of course," Beryl said. "That's how they eat in France. They have chips with everything. Chips and wine. But we're having iced tea."

"I didn't know they had chips with every meal in France," Molly said.

"Well, they do, Mama. They do."

"I like chips," Dominic said.

"I know you do." Beryl opened the bag and served him first...the precious one, the non-judgmental one, the one not yet old enough to know better. "And let me get you a piece of this...*pot-au-feu*."

"You mean, the meat?" he asked.

"Yes, angel," Beryl said, "the meat."

She was having difficulty cutting the meat, so Terry came to her aid. "Sit down. You've been on your feet too much today. Let me do that."

Beryl gladly relinquished the knife and meat fork. She sat down and watched Terry saw into the meat as if it were a block of wood. At last, everyone was served, and Dominic and Duncan's meat was hacked into bite-sized pieces.

Beryl cut off a bite of her meat and popped it into her mouth. The more she chewed, the bigger the meat seemed to get. She glanced around the table. Duncan and Dominic were eating their chips, but it appeared that Molly and Terry were having the same difficulty she was having.

"This isn't fit to eat," Beryl said, when she was finally able to swallow.

"It's fine," Terry said. "Really."

"No, it isn't," Beryl said. "We can't eat this." With a sigh, she got up from the table and got out five bowls. "I've found that granola based cereals are the best bet for an evening meal." She began setting boxes of cereal on the table. "And we have your choice of fruity or chocolatey cereals for dessert. I keep an assortment on hand for just such an emergency."

"We eat cereal a lot," Duncan said.

"I like cereal," Dominic added.

After Terry left, Beryl put a movie on for the boys and made Molly and herself a cup of coffee.
"I need to talk with you, Mama," she said.

Molly raised her brows speculatively. "About a certain sexy teacher?"

"No...not this time." She stirred a spoonful of sugar into her coffee.

"Is it Raife?"

Beryl sighed. "In a way." She went on to explain about Bob March and the way he'd overcharged estates, including August's and Ron's, on executor and legal fees. "Terry thinks Bob might've retained Raife to botch the rope so I'd fall."

Molly took a sip of her coffee. "What do you think?"

"Raife wouldn't do that to me."

"I don't think he would either," Molly agreed, with a shake of her head. She traced the plaid pattern on the place mat with an index finger. "But Terry doesn't know Raife like we do. He's terribly concerned about you."

"Why, Mama? He's made it clear he isn't interested in a relationship."

Molly chuckled. "Not to me, he hasn't."

Beryl decided to set that delicate issue aside and concentrate on the matter at hand. "The reason I wanted to talk with you is...before I reopen some of those estate files--"

"Including August's and Ron's?"

"Possibly." She placed a hand over her mother's. "How do you feel about that?"

Molly stared into her coffee cup before raising her eyes to

Beryl's. "Do you what you have to do. If that greedy low-life gypped my grandbabies, I wanna know about it. And I wanna make him pay for it."

"That's all I needed to know."

Beryl snuggled under her down comforter and reached for the remote. The boys were sleeping, and Molly had gone home. All was quiet and peaceful. As she channel-surfed, she ran across *To Catch a Thief*.

While Grace Kelly lifted her beautiful face to look at Cary Grant's beautiful face, something crashed outside. Beryl muted the television. She could hear someone cursing.

Using only the light from the television, she crept out of bed and down the stairs. She eased back the curtain at the side of the living room window and could see someone's shadow. He moved closer to the porch. Beryl slipped over to the front door. Staying well to the side of the door, she poked her head around to peer out the glass. As she did, she could see a man's silhouette.

She quickly moved back around out of view of the glass. She should call 9-1-1...but how could she get to the phone without him seeing her? She frowned. So what if he did see her? She was calling the police. Except, if it was a robber, he could shoot her through the glass and then come in on the boys.

On the verge of hyperventilation, she flattened her back and arms against the wall and tried to think. She had to be calm. She had to be in control of the situation. She had to be The Flame.

"Beryl? Beryl, it's me, Terry. Let me in."

It took a moment for the voice and the words to register. When they did, Beryl opened the door and slapped Terry against the side of his head.

"Ow! What'd you do that for?"

"Do you realize what time it is?"

"I know it's late, but may I come in? I need to talk with you."

"About what?"

"May I please come in? It's cool out here."

Beryl stepped back and flipped on the living room light. Both she and Terry squinted against the sudden brightness.

Terry was rubbing the back of his left thigh. "Those guys need to put their toys up when they're finished with them. I nearly killed myself when I tripped over a plastic truck."

"Yeah, well, try telling them that. What are you doing here?"

"I was thinking about last night, and I got this craving for ice cream. So I--"

"So you came here?"

"Will you let me finish?" Terry put his fingers against his temples. "If you aren't going to let me talk to you, there's no point in my being here. Would you like me to leave?"

Beryl sat down on the sofa and patted the cushion beside her.

"Thanks," Terry said, accepting the seat she offered. "I was driving back from Dairy Queen when I decided to swing by the station and check on your car."

"Thank you. How is it? Was it still there?"

"Yes, it was. Anyway--"

"All of it or parts of it?"

"All of it. Beryl, I am trying desperately to tell you something."

She rolled her eyes. "Then spit it out. Cary Grant is upstairs waiting for me."

Terry took her by the shoulders. "This is serious, okay. I saw Raife coming out of the station."

"You're right. This is serious. A man was caught at his place of employment. How strange."

He abruptly pushed her away. "Never mind. Okay? Never mind. I won't waste my breath telling you something you obviously don't want to hear."

"Terry, I don't see what the big deal is. Raife was coming out of the station. So what?"

"After hours."

"And you never go by the school after hours?"

"This is different."

"In what way?"

"Look, somebody let you down yesterday...literally. I'm afraid he might've been setting you up for another so-called accident."

"I don't think so, Terry. Raife is my friend. He wouldn't do that to me."

"Wouldn't? Or you don't want to believe that he would?"

"Wouldn't."

"Just be careful, okay?" He cupped her face in his hands.

"Why are you so concerned, teacher?" Beryl teased, leaning closer to him.

"Because those little boys need you, that's why."

Oh. The boys *need me.*

"You're absolutely right. And I need my sleep. The Flame is back in business tomorrow morning." She stood as if to usher him to the door.

He didn't take the hint. "You're resuming production tomorrow?"

"Yes."

"What time do I need to pick you up?"

"You don't. I have transportation to the station. Hmmm. That sounds like one of those old Schoolhouse Rock® ditties." She snapped her fingers. "Transportation station--"

Terry shook his head. "I give up on you then. Goodnight." He turned toward the door. "I will see you in the morning, though. I intend to be at that shoot."

Beryl smiled serenely. "Why, Mr. Goodson, are you this considerate of all your students and their families?"

Terry turned back to face Beryl. "I try to be."

"Ah. How many people's jobs have you visited this week?"

"That's not the point."

"And what is the point?"

"I don't want to see you get hurt."

Funny that should be coming from you, she thought.

"That's very sweet of you," she said. "Goodnight."

"I'll see you in the morning." He took her arm so she could lean on him as they walked to the door. "I'd be glad to carry you up the stairs."

"Would you really? Be glad?"

Ignoring her mocking questions, Terry simply picked her up and took her upstairs to her bedroom. Unlike the last time he'd been in her room, the bed was tantalizingly rumpled, the wardrobe was open displaying the television, and Cary Grant and Grace Kelly were kissing passionately.

"Terry?"

"Yes?"

"Is the real reason you want to come to the shoot tomorrow because I told you I don't wear underwear under the catsuit?"

"No," he answered thickly. "Were you lying?"

"Oh, no. I just wondered if that's why you wanted to come."

He gently lowered her onto the bed. "You drive me insane...you know that?"

"How so?"

"In every conceivable way." He kicked off his loafers and lay down beside her. "You're an incredible woman." He dropped feathery kisses down her neck and pushed the satin burgundy pajama top off her shoulder so he could kiss her there, too.

Beryl felt the explosive desire he could evoke with a single touch. She needed to send him away...now. She wanted more than he was willing to offer--he'd already made that clear. Besides, she'd promised herself that the boys would never see a man in her bed unless he was her husband.

She kissed the top of his head in what she hoped would translate into an act of indifference. "I think it's time for you to show some of that teacher/student consideration."

"What?" Terry asked, still kissing her throat.

"Lock the door on your way out." She felt Terry's body stiffen.

"Sure," he said tightly, quickly getting out of her bed. "Goodnight."

Without a second glance, he was gone.

Beryl closed her eyes and listened to the door open and shut downstairs.

Terry stumbled through the door of his apartment and headed straight for the bedroom. He didn't bother to turn on a light. Why should he? He already knew everything that was there...and everything that wasn't.

He kicked off his shoes and unbuttoned his shirt. Moonlight streamed through the blinds revealing swatches of his unmade bed. He hadn't had time to make it up before leaving for Beryl's house this morning. Man, her bed had felt great...for the scant time he'd been on it.

He tossed the shirt at the hamper he kept beside the dresser. The shirt fell to the side, and Terry decided to retrieve it in the morning...maybe. He stepped out of his pants and kicked them in the vicinity of the hamper.

As he lay down and pulled the crumpled sheets up around him, he thought again of Beryl's bed. Besides the obvious attraction of having her in it, the sheets were crisp, cool and clean, and they smelled of Beryl's perfume. She had an assortment of fluffy pillows along the headboard and even one of those fancy little bolster pillows.

116

He smiled. *My beautiful girl...a cross between a lap dog and a tigress.* The smile faded. *Not that she is my girl. Not really. Her bed felt great. So what? I'm tired. It's a great bed.*

The bed at camp wasn't such a great bed, though. The bedspread had been thin and showing signs of wear. No fluffy pillows either. One flat pillow per twin bed. Period. Yet, even that bed had felt terrific when he'd been on it with Beryl.

He remembered the lunch he'd had with her yesterday. Wow...was that delicious. It was a simple meal, but one of the best he'd had in a long time. He'd had many fancy dinners in dimly lit restaurants with the current date-of-the-month (as his brother had always accused him of having), but they didn't compare to yesterday. Hell, even the cereal they'd had tonight was pretty good.

The food...the laughter...the company and companionship...not only of Beryl but of the boys and Molly, too. He'd left his own family in Memphis when he'd taken the position at Harper Elementary; and though he still spoke with his mom frequently by phone and kept in touch with his brother via e-mail, he missed them. Yesterday and tonight he'd regained his sense of family with Beryl and the boys.

And yet, it was superficial. They weren't his. But they could be. The big "L" word sprang to mind. No way. He wasn't ready to commit to anyone. No indeed.

But if he was, it would be Beryl...and he'd need to take some cooking lessons...for all their sakes.

Terry flung himself over in the bed, feeling frustrated and alone. He needed to get some sleep. He didn't intend to miss a second of that taping tomorrow.

11

There was no sign of Terry at the studio the next morning. Beryl assumed she'd made him angry last night and he'd decided not to come. She brushed aside her disappointment as she sat down in Raife's makeup chair.

"How are you?" she asked.

"I'm fine. It's you I'm concerned about. You sure you're up to this?"

She shrugged. "The show must go on, you know."

"Not at your expense."

"We missed you last night."

"I missed you guys, too."

"And you missed a terrific meal. I made *pot-au-feu* for Terry, Mama, and the boys."

Raife rocked back on his heels and held up his hands. "You? Made *pot-au-feu*?"

"We ended up having cereal."

He closed his eyes, rocked forward and kissed the top of her head. "I've tried. God knows I've tried."

"I guess where cooking is concerned, I'm just unteachable. By the way, when Joe phoned yesterday, I suggested he get an intern to handle the props so you won't have so much responsibility."

"Did you now?" He straightened, pushed her hair away from her face and secured it with a clip.

"Yes.... Do you mind?"

"Why should I?" He began putting foundation on her face with a makeup sponge. "Close your eyes, babe."

"Are you mad at me?"

"No. Close your eyes."

She complied with his directive and decided to let him speak next. The silence nearly wore down her patience before he finished with her makeup and finally spoke.

"You know I didn't intend to let you fall, don't you?" he asked, whisking the clip out of her hair and grabbing a comb.

"Of course, I do."

"Do you? Really?"

"Of course!"

"You don't think anyone tampered with the reel the rope was on?"

"No."

"I do," he said quietly.

"What?"

"We'll talk about it after the shoot. Just be careful and watch what you're doing, okay?"

"Yeah...sure." She frowned at him via the mirror. "You're freaking me out."

"I'm sorry. I don't mean to. It's just...I don't know. I guess Joe's suspicions about me gave me a few suspicions of my own. Just watch yourself."

"Three minutes, people!" Joe shouted. "Let's get into position!"

The script called for The Flame to get up off the floor ("where we last saw her") and chase after those brassy bandits, the Gemstones.

As this could not very well be a foot race, Joe had elected to bring out "the Dynamobile." That was The Flame's vehicle. It was a cardboard cutout resembling a red-orange hotrod, and Beryl sat on a stool and held it up by clutching the steering wheel. Sure, the studio could've gone CG, but Joe liked to keep things old school. Though the Dynamobile wasn't used very often (it was usually kept in the Cinders, The Flame's hideout), it served the purpose when it had to, and it looked as realistic as anything else that was a part of the show.

Naturally, with the Dynamobile being put into play, the Gemstones had needed a vehicle. Upon seeing it, Beryl realized why Raife had been at the station last night.

The Gemstones were escaping in "The Crown Jewels," a huge contraption which looked like a gaudy crown on wheels. A scepter served as a gearshift (as the steering wheel alone was not enough to hold up The Crown Jewels--Beryl thought there was probably a sex joke in there somewhere but didn't have time to figure it out).

On cue, Raife ran the city scene on a screen behind the vehicles and provided the noise so they could roar down the street.

The Flame twisted the steering wheel like mad, looking first this way and that, as she tried to catch up to the Gemstones. Ruby was driving, Opal was manning the gearshift, and Jade was loading her gun. As Jade raised the gun to shoot at The Flame, someone, shouted, "No! Stop!"

To everyone's amazement, Terry sprang onto the set and tackled Jade, demolishing The Crown Jewels in the process.

"Cut!" Joe bellowed. "What's going on here?"

Terry got up, brushed off his clothes, and helped Jade to her feet. "Are you all right?" he asked.

"I'm fine," Jade said in a voice that got Beryl off her stool and to Terry's side.

"Are you crazy?" Beryl asked. "What are you doing?"

"After your last accident," Terry said, with an accusing glance at Raife, "I was afraid that gun might be loaded."

"It is," Jade said, now a bit testy. "With caps."

"Let's see." Terry held out his hand, and Jade handed over the gun.

Terry pointed the gun at the floor and fired. All bark, no bite.

"See?" Jade retrieved her gun.

"How you plannin' on fixin' this?" Joe asked Terry.

"How should I know?"

"I think we should let him finish saving The Flame before we lose too much more air time," Beryl said with a smile.

"How?" Joe asked.

"Improv." Beryl winked. "Improv, my friend."

"Can you?" Joe asked Terry.

"Uh...yeah...sure."

"Let's go then. Places, people! Three...two...one..." He signaled the cameraman.

Beryl once again got out of the hotrod and rushed to Terry's side. "Thanks, but no thanks, mister. I could've taken care of myself."

"Oh, really?" Terry asked, jerking the gun away from Jade and waving it in front of Beryl's face. "You think you're so independent, don't you? You're invincible…you don't need anyone. You're The Flame."

"Oh, no. You're the one who doesn't need anyone. You're--" She frowned. "Who are you?"

The Gemstones were slipping away, but neither The Flame nor the new superhero seemed to notice or care.

"I'm…" Terry cleared his throat. "I…I'll tell you who I am."

Beryl took a step closer. "Please do."

"I'm Batman to your Catwoman. I'm Superman to your Lois Lane." He pulled Beryl to him with his free hand. "And as you are The Flame, I must be the fuse because…" He dropped the gun and put his other arm around Beryl. "…together we are spontaneous combustion." He lowered his mouth to hers.

With a moan, Beryl snaked her arms around his neck and proved the validity of his words.

"Cut! This is a *kid's* show, people!"

Beryl could've argued that point after yesterday, but at the moment, she had her mind on other things. Obviously, so did Terry.

"You really don't wear underwear with this thing, do you?" he whispered.

"Huh-uh."

From the corner of her eye, Beryl saw Jade, a/k/a Irma, shoot her and Terry a scathing look.

"Do you have your own dressing room?" Terry asked, drawing Beryl's full attention back to him.

"I'm afraid not."

"Then maybe we can finish this…conversation…elsewhere."

"Maybe later. As for now, I've got to hustle my behind over to the IRS."

He grinned. "Audit Woman--The Flame. Does your quest for justice ever end?"

"Never." She gave him a quick kiss and then limped off to the dressing room.

I t was a long, mind-searching drive for Terry as he drove to work. When he thought that woman was going to shoot Beryl…that someone might've replaced the gun with a real one…that Beryl might be hurt…he'd panicked. But wouldn't he have done that for anyone whose life he thought was in danger?

Beryl...Beryl...Beryl. When he wasn't with her, he was thinking about her. And not just about how sexy she was and how badly he wanted to make love with her. He wondered how her day was going...what she and the boys were doing...what they were having for dinner--that being a major concern after night before last.

He even wondered if they were doing okay financially. After all, Beryl was working two jobs in order to support two children she hadn't planned for. That must be tough. And yet, nothing seemed to be a hardship for Beryl...merely a new adventure.

And what was he to her? Was he merely a new adventure? Yet, how could he ask her about her feelings when he wasn't sure of his own?

Though Beryl was dressed in a gray silk pantsuit, her hair was still up in The Flame Fount when she arrived at the IRS. She hadn't had time to have Raife do her hair in the elegant chignon he usually put it in for her "serious look," and she didn't have time to bother with it herself either. The hair made her self-conscious today, but she'd try to stay in her office and be as inconspicuous as possible. If anyone said anything, she'd just remind that person that she normally didn't "do Fridays" and that she was only making up the time she missed Wednesday because Hilary took off for a weekend jaunt to the Smokies.

Nancy walked in after the semblance of a knock as Beryl was hanging up the phone. Today Nancy was wearing a tartan plaid jumper with a white turtleneck. She was nearly casual. She even looked attractive. Now, if she'd smile....

"Good--" Nancy faltered as she saw Beryl's hair. "Good morning. What have we here? The new teeny-bopper craze?"

"Actually, it's the hairstyle I wear on the show. I didn't have time to redo it this morning."

"I see." She tossed a file on Beryl's desk. "That needs to be reviewed ASAP."

"No problem." Before Nancy could retreat, Beryl asked, "Have you got a moment?"

"If it's important." Nancy sniffed as she looked at her watch.

"It is. Would you shut the door please?"

As Beryl explained the Bob March situation to Nancy, the woman became more animated than Beryl had ever seen her. For Nancy, that would be little more animation than an electronic Santa ringing a bell in a holiday window display, but it was progress nonetheless.

"I'd like for you to reopen some of those estates," Beryl said. "I don't want Bob March to get away with this."

"Neither do I, and you can bet I'll reopen those estates." Nancy leaned forward and tapped her short, blunt, unpolished nails on the edge of Beryl's desk. "You know this would mean reopening your sister's and her husband's estate too."

"I'm aware of that."

"And that, as that is the case, we'll have to assign someone else to examine the files."

"That's fine. I understand perfectly. In fact, I've already looked over some of them myself and would rather have someone else's input to ensure that I'm not being overly suspicious of March."

"Very well, then," Nancy said, standing and pushing her chair back into the precise spot it had occupied before she'd sat down. "I'll get back with you on this and let you know what comes of it."

"Thank you."

With a nod, Nancy left.

Beryl began working on the file in front of her. She hadn't gotten very far when there was a woodpecker-like knock on her door. Clark? Had to be. Perhaps if she was quiet, he'd assume she was on her coffee break. No such luck.

The woodpecker attempted to drill a hole in her door one more time, and then he opened the door.

"Good morning, Clark," Beryl said.

"Ooooh!" His hands--fingers splayed--went immediately to his chest. "The Flame! You look so wild and sexy with your hair like that. You know, I've never seen you with your hair like this in person."

"Did you need something, Clark?"

"That man on the show this morning, who is he?"

"His name is Terry Goodson."

"Terry Goodson.... Now why does that sound familiar to me?"

"You were scheduled to do his audit. You were sick that day, and I did it."

Clark's eyes widened and he threw up his hands as if she'd just told him this was a hold up. "So now he's stalking you? Oh, my goodness! Poor you...and this is all my fault."

"No, Clark, he--"

"Do they have stalking laws in Tennessee? I know they do in Virginia. My sister Trula was stalked once--she lives in Bristol, on the Virginia side--and she called the police. Every day for a week, a man followed her into her apartment building. She was terrified."

"What happened?"

"When the police came, they told Trula that the man's record was spotless and that he was following her because he lived across the hall." Clark narrowed his eyes. "She's still wary of him, though." He wagged an index finger. "Because you never know. Now, back to this guy who's stalking you. Have you notified the authorities?"

"No. He--"

"Then let's call them right now. I know the dispatch number by heart. They won't allow me to call 9-1-1 anymore unless someone is dying...and if it's Mother, she has to actually *be* dying...not just saying she is." He reached for Beryl's telephone.

"Clark, stop. I know Terry. We became acquainted when Duncan's boys club went on a camping trip."

"Oh." He reluctantly moved his hand away from the phone. "Will he be The Flame's love interest then?"

"I doubt it. He came by the station to see me this morning, and...." She shrugged.

"Became your hero."

"In a roundabout way, I guess you could say that...yes."

"I suppose you want your coloring book back."

"Whatever for? No matter who my hero is, Clark, you'll always be my friend...won't you?"

He nodded. "Of course, I will." He lifted his chin resolutely. "A hero, too, if you ever need one."

"Thank you."

He left without stumping his toe, tripping over either chair, or bumping his head against the door.

Beryl shook her head. Nearly nice Nancy and unclumsy Clark? Could this day get any crazier?

It was a little after three, and Beryl was looking at her watch for the umpteenth time. She had most definitely gotten spoiled to being off on Fridays. Of course, she did the show, but that didn't count. That was like being a little girl and playing dress-up. This was tiring...boring... conducive to a good desk nap.

She was jolted out of her siesta when Nancy pounded two quick thumps on the door and rushed in.

"I've been working on this Bob March affair, and it's terrible," she told Beryl. "You're absolutely right about his charging twelve percent plus legal bills on these estates. The guy is perpetuating a fraud on every estate he administers."

Beryl nodded. "That's what I thought."

"Mum's the word for now, but I've contacted someone at the federal level. I plan to have Mr. March prosecuted to the fullest extent of the law."

"I'm glad," Beryl said, wondering why Nancy was telling her what she already suspected.

"As it stands," Nancy continued, "we'll have enough to convict March without reopening your sister's and your brother-in-law's estate if you'd prefer we don't. We'll also have several thousand dollars in fines and fraud penalties, not to mention the money stolen from heirs of these estates that March will have to pay back with interest."

"I appreciate your concern, Nancy, but I want August's and Ron's estate reopened, too. If my nephews were swindled, I want to know about it; and I want Bob March to repay anything he took from them."

"Thank you," Nancy said. "I'll make sure it's taken care of."

As soon as Beryl heard Nancy's heels tip-tap back down the hall, she looked out the window. Had Hell actually frozen over? It was sunny and beautiful. The leaves were starting to change, and the trees seemed alive with color. There wasn't a snowflake in sight.

Still, Beryl knew the devil must be ice skating out there somewhere.

Speaking of devils, Raife whipped his black Honda into the parking lot. Beryl smiled softly and retrieved her briefcase and crutches. Though it had been a productive day, it had been a long one, and Beryl was ready to go home.

"Hi, baby girl." Raife opened the door for her and tossed her briefcase and crutches into the backseat. "You look beat." He helped her ease into the car. "Why don't I make dinner when I get you home to make up for not being there last night?"

"Sounds wonderful to me."

He went around and got behind the wheel of the car. "Will that be all right with Molly?"

"I'm sure it will. I think she's starting to feel guilty about spending so much time away from Daddy this week."

"That Bill must be some kinda guy."

There was an underlying something in Raife's tone, and Beryl arched a brow suspiciously.

"I mean, he never seems to mind dropping everything and rushing over whenever Molly...and your dad, of course, need him."

Beryl anchored her tongue behind her teeth and continued to level her gaze at him.

Raife shrugged. "He is a widower, isn't he?"

"Yes."

"Well, I'm just saying—"

"Don't. Don't say anything. Remember, those are my parents you're starting to make suggestions about."

"I'm not making suggestions, Beryl. Not the way you mean. I'm only saying that maybe this Bill is in love with your mom and that...someday..."

"Enough, Raife! All right?"

"All right, all right."

It was at that moment that Terry wheeled into the parking lot, saw Raife and Beryl arguing, and lost control to his alter ego—Captain Combustion.

12

Terry spun the car around into an abrupt U-turn. The car's wheels screeched and marred the pavement in protest of their mistreatment.

"What the hell's he doing?" Raife asked.

"Don't ask me. I've been trying to figure out that man since the first time I laid eyes on him, and I'm no closer now than I was then."

Terry's BMW surged up beside Raife's car. Terry pointed to the curb, and yelled, "Pull over!"

Raife pulled over to the curb, whacked the gearshift into park, and loomed up out of the car with his fists planted on his hips. "What are you trying to pull now, Goodson?"

"I'm trying to pull Beryl out of that car before you get her hurt again, that's what I'm trying to pull," Terry said, blasting out of his car.

"Where do you get off accusing me?" Raife demanded, stepping closer to Terry.

Terry didn't step back, and instead took a step toward Raife.

Beryl massaged her temples with her fingertips, certain the two men were about to come to blows.

Upon leaving the building, Clark stopped, cumbersome briefcase in hand, on his way through the parking lot to Mother's Volvo. "Now...now...now...see here," he said to the two irate men. "You brutes are upsetting Beryl."

Terry gave Clark a disparaging glance before turning back to

Raife. "Who's he?"

"Never mind him. We've got something to settle."

Beryl lay her head back against the seat and shut her eyes. Just then, she heard a tap on the window. She reluctantly opened her eyes. To her surprise, Nancy stood there. Beryl lowered the window.

"Shall I take you home?" Nancy asked.

"Oh, would you?"

"I'd be glad to."

Unnoticed by the three men—two of whom were standing toe to toe, and one of whom was nervously standing on the fringe—Beryl got out of Raife's car, retrieved her crutches and briefcase, and walked with Nancy to her gray Mazda sedan.

"What's it like?" Nancy asked her conspiratorially. "To be so sought after, I mean."

Beryl looked back over her shoulder at the Three Stooges and sighed. "Sometimes it just sucks, Nancy."

Was that a dandelion billowing through the air or a snowflake?

Beryl had been home for about ten minutes when Terry and Raife slowly paraded into her driveway. She watched them get out of their cars, look at each other, and then quickly look away. They avoided each other's eyes all the way to her front door.

"Get in here," Beryl said, opening the door before either of them could knock.

"Beryl--"

"Baby girl--"

Hugging her crutches to her with her elbows, Beryl used her hands to waive away their apologies. "You're both sorry. I know. Are you two ready to be rational?"

The men glanced at each other and then nodded.

"Good. Let's go into the dining room then."

"Where are the boys?" Terry asked.

"Molly is picking them up and taking them to McDonald's so the three of us can have a little time to talk."

The men followed Beryl into the dining room. Raife beat Terry to the punch at pulling out Beryl's chair for her, and Terry watched carefully as if Raife might go ahead and pull the chair completely out from under her. When they were seated at Beryl's left and right, she abruptly got to the heart of the matter.

"Terry, let's start with your telling Raife why you suspect he's trying to harm me."

"All right." Terry spoke like a cross between a football coach trying to fire up his team and a district attorney. "You work for Bob March. You're the only person--besides her mother and me--in whom Beryl has confided her suspicions about March. Maybe you decided you could make some extra money by letting him in on--"

"First of all," Raife interrupted, "I work for the station, not Bob March. Just because the man owns shares of the company does not make him my employer. Second--"

"As the prop man, Beryl puts her trust in you every day. Are you loyal enough to her to deserve that trust?"

"Damn straight I am!" Raife flattened his palms against the table and leaned closer to Terry.

"What were you doing outside the station late last night?" Terry asked.

"Completing the Crown Jewels and checking out the props. I've been having some suspicions of my own."

"You mentioned that this morning," Beryl said. "So you don't think my falling was an accident either?"

Raife sighed. "I don't know, babe. I really don't. I'd hate to think Joe would--"

"Joe!"

Raife lifted his hands. "Again, I don't know. I hope not...but he's always close enough that he could've heard you tell me what you think about Bob March...and he could've tampered with the rope reel...and he was awfully quick to accuse me...."

"But why would you think Joe would--"

"For the same reason I suspected Raife," Terry interjected.

"Right." Raife regarded Terry thoughtfully. "I guess we were on the same wavelength after all."

Terry nodded. "Sorry I accused you, Raife."

"It's all right, but now we've got to figure out if I'm as wrong about Joe as you were about me."

"He called me at work this afternoon," Beryl said. "He's dropping by here later with a revised script for Monday." She flashed Terry a wry grin. "Now that Captain Combustion has exploded onto the scene, somebody had to do some major rewrites."

"Please tell me they don't include me," Terry said.

"Of course, they include you. You don't expect to write yourself into a show and then merely disappear, do you?" She laughed.

"Well, I'm not wearing tights."

"Don't look at me," Beryl said, with a nod at Raife. "There's your costume designer."

"Revenge is sweet, you know," Raife said.

"Hey, I said I was sorry."

"Yeah, but you didn't mean it." Raife chuckled. "I'm only kidding. I'll do your costume up right."

"But how about Joe?" Terry asked. "How do we decide what--if anything--he's up to?"

Raife looked at his watch. "If he's dropping the script off on his way home, he has to be here soon."

"If we move our cars into a neighbor's driveway or across the street," Terry said, "it'll look like Beryl is here alone."

"And if he's planning on trying anything, he'll do it then," Raife finished.

"Hi, kid," Joe said, shuffling his body over the threshold and handing Beryl two scripts. "You think lover boy will go for this?"

"I don't know," Beryl said. "We'll see."

"He'd better. He's the one who crashed a live taping, and he's gonna make it right."

"I'm sure he will, Joe."

"What the heck was the matter with him anyway?"

"He was afraid the gun was real." Beryl gestured for Joe to sit down. She could have sworn the sofa winced as he lowered his bulky frame onto it.

"Now, that's ridiculous. Why would I allow a real gun on the set? Into the studio even? I'm not that stupid."

"I know. He and Raife really got spooked over my accident. Neither of them seems to think it was an accident."

"Well, if Raife thinks it wasn't an accident, how does he think it got done? And why?"

"He doesn't know how it got done, but he thinks it has something to do with Bob March."

"Bob? Why would he want you to get hurt in a studio he owns

shares in? If you sue, the money will come from his pocket, too, you know."

"I know." Never the hedger, Beryl said, "I've uncovered some damaging things about Bob during some audits though."

A series of bumps came from the closet. Joe turned in surprise.

"It's the boys," Beryl said. "They're playing hide and seek."

Joe nodded slowly. "So Bob's been taking money under the table?"

"Something like that."

"Doesn't surprise me." He placed his hands on his knees and heaved himself up off the sofa. "You and your beau review your scripts this weekend, and I'll see you both on Monday morning."

"All right, Joe. Thanks."

She waited for Joe to lumber down the front steps and said, "You can come out now."

Raife and Terry burst out of the closet.

"Are you insane?" Raife asked.

"What did you go telling him that for?" Terry asked.

"Look, guys, if March is paying him to try to scare me off his back, Joe already knows what's going on. If not, where was the harm in telling him?" She shrugged. "Besides, wouldn't that have been the perfect opportunity for him to warn me to leave Bob alone?"

"It would have if he hadn't thought 'the boys' were playing hide and seek in the closet," Terry said, with a glare at Raife.

"You're the one who pushed up against me when she blurted out the truth."

"What difference does it make?" Beryl asked. "Whether the boys were here or not, Joe could've lowered his voice and threatened me or told me to back off or something."

"Still--"

Terry didn't get to finish his thought as Molly and the boys blasted into the house.

"Aunt B," Dominic said, running to Beryl's side. "We dot 'Toy Store'! We dot 'Toy Store'!"

"It's 'Toy Story 3'," Duncan corrected, "and it's an awesome movie."

"I'll pop some popcorn before I go," Molly said, dropping a kiss on her daughter's forehead. "Have you eaten, honey?"

"Nah, I'll grab something in a little while. You go on home to Daddy."

"Bill won't mind waiting a few more minutes," Molly said.

Beryl glanced at Raife who was wisely studying his fingernails.

"Nonsense, Mama. I can take care of myself."

"You run on, Molly," Terry said. "I'll make something for the three of us--"

"Count me out," Raife said. "Though I appreciate the offer, I have plans."

"But--"

Raife interrupted Beryl simply by shaking his head. "I have plans."

"Will you stay and watch the movie with us, Uncle Terry?" Dominic asked.

The room held its collective breath at Dominic's slip, until Terry answered, "I'd love to. Just let me fix your aunt and me something to eat, and we'll be right there." He turned to Beryl. "Peanut butter sandwich sound all right?"

"It's either that or cereal," she answered.

"Since I'm cooking, we'll go with the sandwiches. I don't want to venture into your area of expertise."

"Come on, Molly," Raife said. "I'll see you to your car."

Beryl decided that Terry must have designated himself her protector for the weekend because when he left Friday night, he asked her and the boys to have dinner with him on Saturday.

"Can we, Aunt B?" Duncan asked.

"Can we?" Dominic chimed in.

"Sure," Beryl answered.

"And after dinner, would anyone like to go to the arcade in the mall?"

"Yeah!" both boys exclaimed at once.

Terry raised a questioning brow at Beryl.

"Sounds great," she said.

And, thus, the groundwork was laid. As Beryl lay awake in the stillness of her bed Friday night, she stared at a shaft of moonlight on the wall and made yet another futile attempt to figure out the enigma that was Terry Goodson. Could he possibly want to trade his freedom for a family? For them? Had he at last grasped that responsibility was not a bad thing? Or had the events of the past few weeks merely reinforced to him the distressing weight he already equated with responsibility? Was Terry simply doing his part to protect Beryl because a guilty conscience blamed him for her current troubles? After all, if Beryl hadn't performed Terry's audit, she wouldn't have suspected Bob March of any wrongdoing in the first place.

Was Terry falling in love with her? Or was he just being Captain Combustion?

Saturday evening, Beryl didn't want to overdress but wanted to wear something that would snare Terry's attention. After looking through everything in her closet at least twice, she decided on a pair of stonewashed jeans and a turquoise cowl neck sweater. She put on her tennis shoes and decided to go without the crutches tonight. If she needed to, she'd lean on Terry.

His low whistle when she carefully made her way down the stairs told her that she'd succeeded in getting his attention. "You look great."

"You don't look bad, yourself." You don't look bad? He looked fantastic! He wore dark jeans and a black knit turtleneck. The shirt provided a striking contrast to his fair complexion and those "excuse-me-while-I-kiss-the-sky" eyes.

"Anybody up for Italian?" Terry asked.

"How about Nordic?" Beryl asked.

"Excuse me?" Terry asked, raising his brows.

"I said, that sounds perfect." She looked at Dominic and Duncan. "Pizza sound good to you two?"

"Yeah!"

"Sure does!"

Beryl nodded at Terry. "Then let's go."

It was early enough in the evening that Figaro's usual crowd had not yet gathered. Figaro's was popular because it managed to cater to both children and adults without leaning too heavily one way or the other. As soon as they were seated, however, it became apparent to Beryl that the restaurant was too crowded for her peace of mind. Bob March was sitting in the booth directly in front of them.

Beryl gave him a polite nod and then engrossed herself in her menu.

"Is everything okay?" Terry asked quietly.

"Fine. Everything's fine."

"I want meatballs on my pizza," Dominic announced.

"You mean beef," Duncan said. "They don't put meatballs on pizza, do they, Terry?"

"Yes, they do!" Dominic didn't give Terry a chance to answer. "They do put on meatballs!"

"Huh-uh!"

"Uh-huh!"

"They do, don't they, Terry?" Dominic asked.

"I think they do sometimes," Terry said.

Beryl smiled serenely, glad it was not she being tugged into the middle of one of the boys' debates for a change. Debate? More like a taffy pull--with her being the taffy. But it looked like it was Terry's turn to be the taffy.

"See?" Dominic said, chin lifted triumphantly.

"He said sometimes, not all the times." Duncan was determined not to let his younger brother have the last word.

"That's enough, boys," Beryl said.

"Well, well, well…"

Beryl immediately recognized the booming voice and slowly lowered her menu. "Hello, Bob."

"Hi, there." He grinned at the boys. "Howdy, boys."

Both boys stared at him wordlessly. Beryl didn't prod them into speaking. After all, they didn't realize it, but this jerk had stolen money from them.

"Glad to see you're up and around without your crutches today, Beryl," Bob said. His grin disappeared. "You gotta be more careful, girl. You need to be real careful." With that, he tipped his forty-four gallon Stetson at the group at large and waddled away.

Terry opened his mouth, but closed it again when he caught the barely perceptible shake of Beryl's head.

Not here, her expression clearly said. *Not in front of the boys.*

Sunday afternoon, Terry sat alone in his apartment. He looked at the kitchen void of furniture save the two stools pushed up under the island. No pictures adorned the walls. No living room or bedroom suites cluttered up the rooms. He had Uncle Joe's couch and a bed frame and mattress he'd bought at a discount store. Other than his television set, that was about it.

It was peaceful and quiet in his apartment. There were no sounds of anyone else moving about the place...playing games...bickering...trying to cook...laughing.

Yep. His apartment was about as empty as it gets. As empty as his life had been.

He wandered over to the counter and picked up the telephone directory. Finding the listing he wanted, he dialed without hesitation.

"Raife? Terry Goodson here. I need to talk with you."

13

Monday arrived well before Terry wanted it to. He'd been enjoying the weekend and dreading the morning when he'd have to put on a silly costume and make a spectacle of himself in front of that television camera one more time. The first time had been unintentional. He'd been thinking of nothing but Beryl and the possibility that she might get hurt. This was an entirely different matter.

Beryl was already at the station and in costume when Terry got there. Raife stopped fussing with Beryl's hair long enough to hand Terry his costume and usher him into the dressing room. At least, there were no tights.

In fact, Terry had to admit that his costume was pretty snazzy. It was a black, one-piece suit with a hood, and it was spattered with multi-colored "explosions" like a fireworks display. A black, Lone Ranger-type mask completed the ensemble. When Terry stepped out of the dressing room, Beryl winked her approval.

"Everybody get ready to go!" Joe called.

Beryl and Terry took their places.

"Quiet! In three...two...one...." Joe nodded at the cameraman who began rolling the film.

"Who are you?" The Flame asked Captain Combustion.

"Someone who has known you forever, Bess Keene."

"B-bess Keene? What are you talking about?"

He chuckled. "You know exactly what I'm talking about. You do know who you are, don't you, Bess?"

"Of course, I know who I am." She paced away from him then spun back around to look at him. "But you haven't answered my question. Who are you?"

"I'm Captain Combustion, and we're the same, you and I. We come from the same place."

"You're from--?

"The Isle of Youth...yes."

Beryl's eyebrows bumped her hairline. That was an ad-lib! He was supposed to have said he was from Mitoblia! She picked up her next line. "Perhaps so...but I left that life behind me."

Captain Combustion smiled. "Not entirely. A part of it will live inside you always."

The Flame inclined her head. "That is true...and yet, I have moved on. I have a life here. I have responsibilities."

"I want to share those responsibilities."

Beryl's jaw dropped. *What is he doing? He's supposed to be asking me to go back to Mitoblia with him so I can refuse and he'll no longer be part of the show. Why on Earth would he change horses in the middle of the stream? Is he vying for an Emmy here?* She looked helplessly out at Joe who had his eyes closed and was rubbing the bridge of his nose.

"I mean it, Bess," Captain Combustion continued. "After rescuing you from the Gemstones the other day, I went back to the Isle of Youth and...and nothing was the same. The things I thought mattered don't anymore. You matter. You and the b--b--" He was obviously groping for a word. "--burglars you catch....I want to...to catch them, too."

"I...I'm not sure I understand you, Captain Combustion."

Suddenly, Jade leaped out onto the set. A gun trembled in her outstretched hands. "This time I'm getting rid of you for good, Flame!"

"Get that thing away from me, Jade." The Flame broke away from Captain Combustion and slapped Jade's hands. "What are you doing here, anyway? The Gemstones are supposed to be in jail."

"Maybe the Gemstones are in jail, but I'm not. And I'm not playing!" She raised the gun again.

The Flame was getting sick of everyone ad-libbing and not sticking to the script. It was throwing her off. She ground her teeth.

"Get that out of my face, Jade, you greedy jackal. If you dare aim that weapon at me one more time, I'm shoving it up your nose." She smacked Jade's arms down again, this time using more force than was probably necessary.

A loud boom permeated the set.

The Flame looked down and saw the splintered floor in front of Jade. With a gasp, she dived, head-butting Jade squarely in the stomach and knocking her to the ground. The gun went off again, this time shattering a light bulb above the set.

"Everybody get down!" The Flame yelled, straddling Jade and beating the woman's hand against the floor until she released the gun. The Flame stood and kicked the gun safely out of Jade's grasp.

Sputtering, Jade staggered to her feet. "You won't get away with this."

The Flame rolled her eyes. "That's enough, Jade."

"It'll never be enough!" She advanced upon The Flame, her hands curling into fists.

The Flame took one step forward, came around with a right hook, and knocked Jade back onto the floor. "I said, that's enough."

"Biff! Pow!" Raife exclaimed in his voice-over voice. "That's showing that bimbotic bauble! She'll know not to cross The Flame again! But what of Captain Combustion? Tune in tomorrow, kids, for another exciting episode of *The Flame*."

"Wrap!" Joe yelled. "What the hell is going on here?"

"Call the police, Joe," Beryl said. "She just tried to kill me."

"Not me! I mean, he paid me to do it!" Jade/Irma finally quit fighting and lay sobbing on the floor.

"Are you all right?" Terry asked Beryl.

"I'm fine."

"I would've intervened, but I thought the cat fight was part of the act."

"It ought to be, considering our audience's demographics." Beryl lifted her chin. "But no intervention was necessary, thank you. The Flame fights her own battles."

"And she fights them well," he agreed with a nod. "But wouldn't it be nice to have some backup once in a while?"

"You'd have been there if I'd really needed you. Wouldn't you?"

"You know I would have."

R aife was supposed to have been at Beryl's house by noon to work on coloring books. By one-thirty, Beryl was getting worried. She'd left him three voicemails and had sent half a dozen texts. She'd called the station and was told that Raife had left about ten a.m. In between her attempts to find Raife, Nancy called to let Beryl know that Bob March had been arrested.

"He's free on bond, though," Nancy said, "so I wanted to call and let you know. You might want to exercise a little extra caution."

"Thanks. Bob probably thinks I performed the audits."

"Probably. But he doesn't know anything for sure."

"True. By the way, who did do them?"

"Clark."

Beryl chuckled. Clark was clumsy, but he was also a thorough, intelligent auditor. "Good choice. Just don't tell him Bob might be a threat, though--it'll make his nose bleed."

Nancy laughed. "I won't."

As soon as they finished their conversation, Beryl called Molly.

"Hey, Mama, I need a favor. What else is new, huh?"

"Nonsense. What do you need?"

"Could you pick the boys up from school this afternoon and take them to your house? I'll pick them up as soon as I can."

"Is anything wrong?"

"I hope not. Raife was supposed to be here at noon and it's--" She looked at her watch. "--two now, and I can't reach him on his cell."

"That's certainly not like Raife."

"No, it isn't." Beryl sighed. "Plus, Nancy Carruthers called me. Bob March has been arrested but is out on bond."

"You don't think he might've done something to Raife, do you?"

"No...I don't think so. He might've tried to use his pull with the shareholders to get Raife fired or something underhanded like that, but I don't think he would physically hurt Raife. Besides, why would he go after Raife? Why not me?"

"I'd say the place to start looking for Raife might be the station. Maybe he got tied up doing something and lost track of time."

"That was my initial thought, too, but when I called there, the receptionist said she hadn't seen him."

"Maybe he just isn't where he's usually at. Go there first and see if you can find him."

"Will do. Thanks for taking care of the boys."

"My pleasure."

Beryl hung up the phone and hurried into the kitchen to grab her purse. Before she could get out the door, the phone rang.

"Yes?" she answered anxiously.

"Beryl, thank heavens you're home safe and sound."

"Clark...hi. Look, I don't mean to be rude or anything, but I'm on my way out the door."

"I don't know if that's such a good idea. I'm calling to warn you that Bob March is on the loose."

"I know. Nancy called me."

"Since he did your sister's estate, he might think you're behind some sort of plot to do him in."

"Well, in a way, I am."

Clark gasped. "That's right. You are."

"I'll be fine, Clark. Thanks for calling, and I'll see you tomorrow."

"By the way," he said, before she could hang up, "I saw your tangle with Jade this morning. Ooooh, it was delicious!"

Beryl closed her eyes and ground her teeth. "Thanks, but I--"

"Of course, Mother came in as the show was ending and thought I was watching a porno flick. She--"

"I've really gotta go, Clark. Bye." She hung up before he could say anything else and hurried out the door.

Though he didn't have bus duty, Terry waited and watched while the parents picked their children up that afternoon. He was pleasantly surprised to see that Molly arrived to pick up Duncan. Beryl must have called and asked her mother to watch the children so the two of them could have some time alone this evening. She'd read his message this morning loud and clear. He smiled, watched Molly's Explorer wind around the loop and back out to the highway, and rushed to his car. He had an evening to plan for.

R aife wasn't at the station. No one had seen him since that morning. He wasn't at his apartment either.

Beryl was heading back toward her house when she met Raife. Each slammed on their brakes, backed up and put down their windows.

"Where've you been?" they asked each other in unison.

"Where've *I* been?" Beryl asked. "You're the one who was supposed to be at my house at noon."

"But the receptionist at the station said you'd left word for me to meet you at the coffee house. I've been there since noon."

"Why didn't you call me?"

"For some reason, I didn't have cell service there. And while I was waiting for you, Bob March walked by and started asking me what you knew. I told him I had no idea what he was talking about, and he said that was all right that he'd find out what you knew."

"March! He left that message, Raife. He set us up!"

"Holy deceit and deviation, Flame! You're right!"

A horn blared, the protest of a motorist who had pulled up behind Beryl and had finally lost patience with them.

"To the Cinders! I mean, my house." Beryl spurred the Camaro forward and left the impatient motorist in her wake.

T erry was whistling when he arrived at Beryl's house. There was a strange car in the driveway--a white Cadillac with bullhorns mounted in the grill--but he didn't let that deter him. He tucked the long, slender white box under his arm and was still whistling when he got to the front door.

It was there that the whistling stopped. The front door was ajar, and Terry got the feeling that something wasn't quite right.

He stepped inside the darkening living room and flipped on a light. There were papers strewn everywhere. Books had been flung off the bookshelf. The cushions had been tossed off the couch and were scattered about the room.

Terry was certain this was not a mess the boys had made.

Suddenly, he was shoved from behind and took a tumble over the coffee table. The red roses in the box he'd been holding scattered around him, and he stuck his finger on a thorn as he tried to stand up.

As Bob March ambled toward Terry with his meaty hands balled into fists, Molly shot through the door and pounced on

Bob's back. Terry struggled to his feet, now uncertain as to whether or not to punch March because he was afraid he'd miss and hit Molly.

Or worse, what if he knocked March down and the big oaf squashed Molly? Terry watched Molly claw at March's eyes and watched March try unsuccessfully to dislodge the small but tenacious woman. He then watched in amazement as a tall, thin man he'd never seen before calmly entered the living room and lifted Molly off Bob March's back.

"Ralph!"

Apparently Molly was surprised, too.

"Don't even think about hurting my wife," Ralph Madison said during the most lucid moment he'd had in two years.

It was at that precise moment that Clark made his dramatic entrance brandishing an antique sword.

"Don't anyone move," Clark cried, "or I'll impale you!"

"Not with my Grandpappy's Civil War sword, you won't!"

The protest came from a rounded square of a woman who reminded Terry of a Grandma from a Fisher Price® play set.

"Back off, Mother," Clark growled.

"Well!"

Beryl pulled the car onto the grass, as there wasn't any more space in the driveway. She got out, leaving the door open, and ran to Molly's Explorer where she could see that Duncan and Dominic were waiting.

"What's going on?" she asked.

Each child launched into his own hyper narrative. Raife pulled in and promised to stay with the boys, so Beryl charged into the house.

Her steps faltered at the scene before her. "What the hell--?"

"Beryl Anastasia, watch your language."

Beryl's mouth dropped. "Daddy?" She looked at Molly. "Mama?"

"So," began an older woman with steel gray hair flattened to her head, "you must be the vixen who has driven my poor son to such foolishness."

Molly squared her shoulders. "I doubt anyone would have to drive your son to foolishness. Or you either, for that matter. It appears to me the two of you have made a home for yourselves there."

"Well! It's easy to see that the daughter gets it from her mother."

"You wanna take this out back?" Molly asked. Her adrenaline was pumping and the fight hadn't gone out of her yet.

"Mama!" Beryl then looked to Terry, who seemed to be the sanest person at this gathering at the moment. "Has anyone called the police?"

"I'll do that right now."

"No need," Clark announced triumphantly. "I called them on the way over.... Though, on second thought, someone else might want to call and confirm." He dared not glance away from Bob March who might make a dash for it, even though there was a possibly sharp, though more probably dull, sword dangerously close to his chest. Doubtless it could scratch him or cause a nasty bruise, but you never know what a desperate criminal will risk in order to escape. "Remember what I told you the other day about the police asking me not to call?"

"Yes, Zorro, I do," Beryl answered. "Terry, could you please go ahead and call 9-1-1?"

"I sure will."

"Just what happened here?" Beryl asked.

"It appears Mr. Goodson happened by and caught Mr. March in the act of rifling through your belongings in an attempt to see what evidence the IRS had against him," Clark explained. "Little did he know that it was I whose audits put an end to his double dealings."

"Hmmm. And who brought the roses?"

"I did," Terry said, replacing the telephone receiver. "The police are on their way."

"Thank you...and thank you for the roses. Any special occasion?"

"I was planning to ask you to dinner."

"Are you still? Planning to ask me, I mean?"

"Of course."

"That sounds terrific. I'd love to."

"Trollop," muttered Mother Samuels.

"You and me..." Molly was jabbing the air toward the kitchen with one blunt thumb. "Out back...right now, battle axe."

"Let it go, Mama," Beryl said, kissing Molly on top of the head. "Let it go."

"Who are these people?" Ralph asked, to no one in particular.

"Smile, Daddy, we're on 'Family Feud.'"

Ralph frowned and shook his head. "That man better had not kiss your mother."

Terry took Beryl by the hand and led her into his apartment building.

"Nice building," Beryl said. "This is the first time I've ever been to your apartment." She smiled. "Though from what you've told me, there isn't much to see."

"That's true. I'm sorry I forgot my wallet." He placed the key in the lock. "But I want to take you someplace nice, so…."

The statement hung in the air as Terry pushed the door open and flipped on the light.

Beryl walked inside and looked around the living room. In a corner of the room was a television. A few feet in front of the television was a dilapidated sofa that looked as if it had been dragged through a mud hole. "Oh, sweetheart, you weren't exaggerating, were you?"

He chuckled. "No. Not at all."

"Something smells good, though," she said. "Like--" She closed her eyes and inhaled the aroma again. "I don't know. Is that sage? Garlic, maybe? One of your neighbors must be cooking."

"Your nose isn't bionic or something, is it, Flame?" He crossed the room and turned on the kitchen light. "I mean, if you're smelling the neighbors' food, you might not appreciate ours."

"Ours?" Beryl took a tentative step toward the kitchen. "You're cooking?"

"That's right."

She took a step closer. "I never dreamed you could cook."

"I couldn't until yesterday. In fact, this is my first attempt."

"Your…your first attempt."

He smiled. "My first attempt…but an attempt immediately following my first cooking lesson, so I'm feeling pretty confident."

When Beryl remained rooted to the floor, Terry strode back into the living room, put an arm around her shoulders and propelled her into the kitchen.

"I was brave enough to try your *pot-au-feu*," he said. "It's--"

"But you didn't know how bad I was at cooking."

"--the least you can do to try my crock pot *coq au vin*."

"Crock pot *coq au vin*?" Beryl echoed. "That's one of Raife's specialties."

"I know."

"Hey, wait a minute." Anchoring one fist on her hip, she turned and reproached Terry with a glare. "You lied to me."

"I did not."

"You did so. You told me the only furniture you had in your kitchen were two stools pushed up under the island." She swept her arm across the room to encompass a black wrought iron bistro set and a baker's rack. "What do you call those?"

"New additions." Terry pulled out one of the bistro chairs and nodded for her to sit.

Beryl moved against the chair as if he were about to pull it away or drop a snake into it, and cautiously lowered herself into a seated perch. Something about this entire situation was making her uncomfortable, and she wanted to be ready to make a run for it if need be.

"You see," Terry continued, "I called Raife yesterday, explained my dilemma, and he agreed wholeheartedly to help me out. The new furniture is--" He held up an index finger. "--one, the best we could do--or rather *he* could do--on short notice and--" The middle finger joined the first. "Two, we decided to be practical."

"Practical, how?"

Terry knelt and took her hands in his. "Practical in that it would be stupid for me to run out and buy a great deal of furniture for a house that is already furnished." He ignored the slackening of her jaw. "So, Raife pointed out that everyone needs a baker's rack in the kitchen and that we can always use the bistro set on the patio."

"So you and Raife are cooking and buying furniture together? What's up with that? Are you getting married?"

"I hope so. Stay right where you are."

Beryl couldn't have moved at that moment if her feet had caught fire. Terry retrieved a small blue box from the kitchen counter. Once again, he knelt before her. This time instead of taking both hands, however, he took only one. The left one.

"Beryl, I love you. I realize that settling down means more than buying furniture and learning to cook, but I hope it shows you that I'm sincere. I want us to make a life together." He flipped the box open. "Will you marry me?"

"Of course, I will. I think I've loved you since I watched you align your planets." She laughed through her tears as he slipped the ring onto her finger.

"Perfect fit," he said.

"We are, aren't we? At least, I think we are."

Terry frowned his confusion at her statement.

Beryl jerked her head toward the crock pot. "The chicken can wait, can't it?"

"Sure."

She slipped her arms around his neck. "Then let's go make sure we're a perfect fit."

His teasing smile answered her own as he lifted her into his arms. "Your wish is my command." He lowered his head to capture her mouth in a searing kiss.

He carried her into his bedroom and lay her on the bed, which had been freshly made and strewn with red rose petals before he'd left for her house earlier.

"Oh, Terry," she breathed, touched by all he had done to impress upon her his sincerity. "I love you."

"I never knew it was possible to love someone the way I love you," Terry said, rolling up onto his elbow to look at her.

Beryl smiled softly. "Are you sure about this? Being the spouse of a crime-fighter is not an easy life."

He grinned. "From what I saw at your house earlier, being an IRS agent is no piece of pie."

She giggled. "Was I dreaming, or was Clark there with a sword?"

"Oh, he was there…right along with Mother."

They laughed.

"That's why I'm marrying you, sweetheart," he said. "I'm tired of the boring bachelor life."

"Well, I can promise you'll never have to suffer from boredom again." She kissed him and let her eyes drift shut.

"Oh, no, you don't," he said. "You're not about to fall asleep on me until we've had some of that chicken that I've been slaving over."

He got up and went into the kitchen. Beryl gave his tight butt an admiring glance and smiled at their unabashed intimacy. It was as if they had been lovers forever. And, somehow, she supposed they had. It was as if Terry Goodson had been made for her, and vice versa.

He returned to the bedroom carrying a platter of chicken, two forks, and a bottle of white wine. Over the neck of the bottle were two paper cups.

He saw Beryl's eyes light on the cups and shrugged. "You have glasses, don't you?"

"Yes, dear, we have glasses."

To Beryl's surprise and delight, the chicken was delicious.

"Sorry we don't have any side dishes or dessert to go with the *coq au vin*," he said. "As I said, yesterday was only my first lesson."

Beryl smiled. "I have everything I need. Everything."

Epilogue

The morning of July 1 dawned sultry, and by eleven a.m., there was a haze that arose to meet the eye wherever you looked...especially the pavement. Although the tiny church had the door to the vestibule open and every fan available running, it was still muggy. Beryl was thankful for her sleeveless, white satin gown and pitied the guys in their black tuxes. Still, it wasn't raining. All her life, Beryl had pessimistically predicted that it would be her luck to have a torrential downpour on her most important of days.

Her father had died soon after the ruckus with Bob March. He'd gone to bed one night in early November and hadn't awakened. The coroner said that his heart had simply stopped beating. Molly was certain that her beloved Ralph was in Heaven, and it was that conviction that had helped her and the rest of the family move on. Molly Madison had a strength borne of an unshakable faith.

Raife had been right about Bill. He'd supported Molly through her time of grief, and now they were going to dinner, the movies, and ice cream socials like a couple of teenagers. But that was all right. Bill had lost a spouse, too. He knew the pain...the loneliness. He'd also been a dear friend to Ralph. Why shouldn't he and Molly find happiness together?

The first notes of "The Wedding March" rang out over the whirring of the fans, and Beryl smiled reassuringly at the handsome young men who were about to escort her down the aisle.

"You're two of the best looking men I've ever seen," she whispered.

Duncan and Dominic drew themselves up as tall as they could, pulled in their stomachs and jutted out their chests. Then they collectively let out their breath and led her to the other most handsome man she'd ever seen.

The ceremony was beautiful but blessedly brief, and then everyone moved into the reception hall. After having cake and punch, throwing the garter (caught by Raife) and tossing the bouquet (caught by Raife), Beryl and Terry disappeared to change into their honeymoon clothes. No one was all that surprised to see them emerge as The Flame and Captain Combustion. Naturally, Raife did a voice over for the wedding video.

"And now The Flame and Captain Combustion will go forth together righting wrongs, overcoming injustice, liberating the oppressed, scorching evil, charring cruelty, searing tyranny, and igniting fear in the hearts of even the coldest of criminals…but not until after the honeymoon."

AUTHOR'S NOTE

Dear Reader:

I hope you enjoyed *The Flame*. It's a book I originally wrote almost twenty years ago! But I couldn't get these characters out of my head, so I revisited them, revised their story a bit, and repackaged it for my readers. If you're familiar with my cozy mysteries, you'll see that this romantic suspense is a departure from that genre. Still, I hope you enjoyed it.

Please let me know what you thought about *The Flame*—what you liked, what you didn't like, whether or not you'd like to see more of the Goodson family. I'd love your feedback. My email address is gayle@gayletrent.com.

Also, as you probably know, reviews are hard to come by. You, the reader, have the power to make or break a book. If you have time, please visit my author page on Amazon (amzn.to/1S9cIXB) and leave a review of *The Flame*. Whether you loved it or hated it, I'd still appreciate your opinion.

Thank you for reading *The Flame* and spending time with me, Beryl, and all the gang in Harper!

Best wishes,

Gayle

ABOUT THE AUTHOR

Gayle Trent (and pseudonym Amanda Lee) writes the Daphne Martin Cake Decorating series, the Myrtle Crumb mystery series, and the Embroidery Mystery series. The cake decorating series features a heroine who is starting her life over in Southwest Virginia after a nasty divorce. The Embroidery Mystery series features a heroine who recently moved to the Oregon coast to open an embroidery specialty shop. She also writes the Down South Café mystery series under the name Gayle Leeson.

Please visit Gayle online at http://www.gayletrent.com or at http://www.gayleleeson.com.

GAYLE TRENT